In praise of C. S. Forester
and *The African Queen*

"I recommend Forester to every literate I know."
— Ernest Hemingway

"The *African Queen* was certainly no lady in Kipling's sense. . . .
The *Queen* was probably as ugly, incompetent, and dilapidated
a thirty-foot launch as one would be likely to find afloat. . . .
But under the deft hand of C. S. Forester she becomes the
instrument of high adventure."
— Percy Hutchison, *New York Times Book Review*

"*The African Queen* is an excellent and exciting novel of
action. . . . Here is somebody who has an undeniable gift for
telling a rattling yarn but who tells it in a clean, direct, and sup-
ple prose — sound prose, without affectation or bravado.
Forester can construct a tight and exciting plot. . . . He can
handle history with vivid accuracy and yet never bog down in
historical detail. . . . And in spite of success, Forester's books
still stay unpredictable — which is one of the essential virtues
of C. S. Forester."
— Stephen Vincent and Rosemary Benet,
  New York Herald Tribune

"Mr. Forester very likely has never seen Central Africa, and
knows of the River Uganda merely by hearsay, but he can cre-
ate an atmosphere that is what the fiction lover demands."
— Amy Lovemen, *Saturday Review of Literature*

"C. S. Forester is one of the great masters of narrative."
— *San Francisco Chronicle*

A Note about Cecil Scott Forester
and *The African Queen*

C. S. Forester (1899–1966) was an accomplished biographer, journalist, and sometime screenwriter, as well as the author of many popular novels, including *The African Queen, The Barbary Pirates, The General, The Good Shepherd, The Gun, The Last Nine Days of the "Bismarck,"* and *Rifleman Dodd*. But Forester is probably best known as the creator of Horatio Hornblower, a British naval genius of the Napoleonic era, whose exploits and adventures on the high seas Forester chronicled in a series of eleven acclaimed historical novels.

Born Cecil Louis Troughton Smith in Cairo, Egypt, C. S. Forester grew up in England. After a brief stint as a poet, he was able to devote himself exclusively to his writing thanks to the great success of the stage and screen versions of his novel *Payment Deferred* (which also helped launch Charles Laughton's career as an actor).

Equal parts adventure and romance, Forester's *The African Queen* has won the hearts of generations of readers and moviegoers. The novel received both critical and popular acclaim when it first appeared in 1932; the legendary film, based on the novel, was released in 1951. Directed by John Huston, starring Katharine Hepburn and Humphrey Bogart, the film won Bogart his sole Academy Award and went on to become one of the most popular films of all time.

At the start of World War II Forester traveled on behalf of the British government to America, where he produced propaganda encouraging the United States to remain on Britain's side. After the war, he remained in America and made Berkeley, California, his home. Forester died in 1966 while writing the last of the Hornblower novels, *Hornblower During the Crisis.*

The African Queen

By C. S. Forester

The Hornblower Saga

MR. MIDSHIPMAN HORNBLOWER

LIEUTENANT HORNBLOWER

HORNBLOWER AND THE *HOTSPUR*

HORNBLOWER DURING THE CRISIS

HORNBLOWER AND THE *ATROPOS*

BEAT TO QUARTERS

SHIP OF THE LINE

FLYING COLOURS

COMMODORE HORNBLOWER

LORD HORNBLOWER

ADMIRAL HORNBLOWER IN THE WEST INDIES

Also

RIFLEMAN DODD

THE GUN

THE PEACEMAKER

THE AFRICAN QUEEN

THE GENERAL

TO THE INDIES

THE CAPTAIN FROM CONNECTICUT

PAYMENT DEFERRED

THE SHIP

THE SKY AND THE FOREST

RANDALL AND THE RIVER OF TIME

THE BARBARY PIRATES

THE NIGHTMARE

THE GOOD SHEPHERD

THE AGE OF FIGHTING SAIL

THE LAST NINE DAYS OF THE *BISMARCK*

The
African Queen

C. S. Forester

BACK BAY BOOKS
LITTLE, BROWN AND COMPANY
NEW YORK BOSTON LONDON

BACK BAY BOOKS/LITTLE, BROWN AND COMPANY
HACHETTE BOOK GROUP
1290 AVENUE OF THE AMERICAS, NEW YORK, NY 10104
WWW.HACHETTEBOOKGROUP.COM

ORIGINALLY PUBLISHED IN HARDCOVER IN THE UNITED STATES
BY LITTLE, BROWN AND COMPANY
REISSUED IN PAPERBACK BY BACK BAY BOOKS, NOVEMBER 2000

BACK BAY BOOKS IS AN IMPRINT OF LITTLE, BROWN AND
COMPANY. THE BACK BAY BOOKS NAME AND LOGO ARE
TRADEMARKS OF HACHETTE BOOK GROUP, INC.

ISBN 978-0-316-28910-8
LIBRARY OF CONGRESS CONTROL NO. 83-83340

TEXT DESIGN BY MERYL SUSSMAN LEVAVI/DIGITEXT

The
African Queen

Chapter 1

ALTHOUGH she herself was ill enough to justify being in bed had she been a person weak-minded enough to give up, Rose Sayer could see that her brother, the Reverend Samuel Sayer, was far more ill. He was very, very weak indeed, and when he knelt to offer up the evening prayer the movement was more like an involuntary collapse than a purposed gesture, and the hands which he raised trembled violently. Rose could see, in the moment before she devoutly closed her eyes, how thin and transparent those hands were, and how the bones of the wrists could be seen with almost the definition of a skeleton's.

The damp heat of the African forest seemed to be intensified with the coming of the night, which closed in upon them while they prayed. The hands which Rose clasped together were wet as though dipped in water, and she could feel the streams of sweat running down beneath her clothes as she knelt, and forming two little pools at the backs of her bent knees. It was this sensation which helped most to reconcile Rose's conscience to the absence, in this her approaching middle age, of her corset — a garment without which, so she had always been taught, no woman of the age of fourteen and up-wards ever appeared in public. A corset, in fact, was quite an impossibility in Central Africa, although Rose had resolutely put aside, as promptings of the evil one, all the thoughts she had occasionally found forming in her mind of wearing no underclothing at all beneath her white drill frock.

Under the stress of this wet heat that notion even re-turned at this solemn moment of prayer, but Rose spurned it and bent her mind once more with anguished intensity to the prayer which Samuel was offering in his feeble voice and with his halting utterance. Samuel prayed for heavenly guidance in the ordering of their lives, and for the forgiveness of their sins. Then, as he began to utter his customary petition for the blessing of God upon the mission, his voice faltered more and more. The mission, to which they had given their lives, could hardly be said to exist, now that Von Hanneken and his troops had descended upon the place and had swept off the entire village, converts and heathen alike, to be sol-diers or bearers in the Army of German Central Africa, which he was assembling. Livestock and poultry, pots and pans and foodstuffs, all had been taken, even the portable chapel, leaving only the mission bungalow standing on the edge of the deserted clearing. So the weakness vanished from Samuel's voice as he went on to pray that the awful calamity of war which had descended upon the world would soon pass away, that the slaughter and destruction would cease, and that when they had regained their sanity men would turn from war to universal peace. And with the utterance of the last of his petition Samuel's voice grew stronger yet, as he prayed that the Almighty would bless the arms of England, and carry her safely through this the severest of all her trials, and would crown her efforts with victory over the godless militarists who had brought about this disaster. There was a ring of fighting spirit in Samuel's voice as he said this, and an Old Testament flavour in his speech, as another Samuel had once prayed for victory over the Amalekites.

"Amen! Amen! Amen!" sobbed Rose with her head bowed over her clasped hands.

They knelt in silence for a few seconds when the prayer was finished, and then they rose to their feet. There was still just light enough for Rose to see Samuel's white-clad figure and his white face as he stood there swaying. She made no move to light the lamp. Now that German Central Africa was in arms against England no one could tell when next they would be able to obtain oil, or matches. They were cut off from all communication with the world save through hostile territory.

"I think, sister," said Samuel, faintly "that I shall retire now."

Rose did not help him to undress — they were brother and sister and strictly brought up, and it would have been impossible to her unless he had been quite incapable of helping himself — but she crept in, in the dark after he was in bed, to see that his mosquito curtains were properly closed round him.

"Good night, sister," said Samuel. Even in that sweltering heat his teeth were chattering.

She herself went back to her own room and lay on her string bed in a torment of heat, although she wore only her thin nightdress. Outside she could hear the noise of the African night, the howling of the monkeys, the shriek of some beast of prey, and the bellow of crocodiles down by the river, with, as an accompaniment to it all — so familiar that she did not notice it — the continuous high-pitched whine of the cloud of mosquitoes outside her curtains.

It may have been midnight before she fell asleep, moving uneasily in the heat, but it was almost dawn when she awoke. Samuel must have been calling to her. Bare-footed, she hurried out of her bedroom and across the living room into Samuel's room. But if Samuel had been sufficiently conscious to call to her he was not so now. Most of what he was saying seemed unintelligible. For a moment it appeared as if he was explaining the failure of his life to the tribunal before which he was so soon to appear.

"The poor mission," he said, and — "It was the Germans, the Germans."

He died very soon after that, while Rose wept at his bedside. When her paroxysm of grief passed away she slowly got to her feet. The morning sun was pouring down upon the forest and lighting the deserted clearing, and she was all alone.

The fear which followed her grief did not last long. Rose Sayer had not lived to the age of thirty-three, had not spent ten years in the Central African forest, without acquiring a capable self-reliance to add to the simple faith of her religion. It was not long before a wild resentment against Germany and the Germans began to inflame her as she stood in the quiet bungalow with the dead man. She told herself that Samuel would not have died if his heart had not been broken by the catastrophe of Von Hanneken's requisitions. It was that which had killed Samuel, the sight of the labours of ten years being swept away in an hour.

Rose told herself that the Germans had worse than Samuel's death upon their souls. They had injured the work of God; Rose had no illusion how much Christianity would be left to the converts after a campaign in the forest in the ranks of a native army of which ninety-nine men out of a hundred would be rank heathen.

Rose knew the forest. In a vague way she could picture a war fought over a hundred thousand square miles of it. Even if any of the mission converts were to survive, they would never make their way back to the mission — and even if they should, Samuel was dead.

Rose tried to persuade herself that this damage done to the holy cause was a worse sin than being instrumental in Samuel's death, but she could not succeed in doing so.

From childhood she had been taught to love and admire her brother. When she was only a girl he had attained the wonderful, almost mystic distinction of the ministry, and was invested in her eyes with all the superiority which that implied. Her very father and mother, hard devout Christians that they were, who had never spared the rod in the upbringing of their children, deferred to him then, and heard his words with respect. It was due solely to him that she had risen in the social scale over the immeasurable gap between being a small tradesman's daughter and a minister's sister. She had been his housekeeper and the most devoted of his admirers, his most faithful disciple and his most trusted helper, for a dozen years. There is small wonder at her feeling an un-Christian rancour against the nation which had caused his death.

And naturally she could not see the other side of the question. Von Hanneken, with no more than five hundred white men in a colony peopled by a million Negroes, of whom not more than a few thousand even knew they were subjects of the German flag, had to face the task of defending German Central Africa against the attacks of the overwhelming forces which would instantly be directed upon him. It was his duty to fight to the bitter end, to keep occupied as many of the enemy as possible for as long as possible, and to die in the last ditch, if necessary, while the real decision was being fought out in France. Thanks to the British command of the sea, he could expect no help whatever from outside; he must depend on his own resources entirely, while there was no limit to the reënforcements which might reach the enemy. It was only natural, then, that with German military thoroughness he should have called up every man and woman and child within reach, as bearers or soldiers, and that he should have swept away every atom of food or material he could lay his hands on.

Rose saw no excuse for him at all. She remembered she had always disliked the Germans. She remembered how, on her first arrival in the colony with her brother, German officialdom had plagued them with inquisitions and restrictions, had treated them with scorn and contempt, and with the suspicion which German officials would naturally evince at the intrusion of a British missionary into a German colony. She found she hated their manners, their morals, their laws, and their ideals — in fact, Rose was carried away in the wave of international hatred which engulfed the rest of the world in August, 1914.

Had not her martyred brother prayed for the success of British arms and the defeat of the Germans? She looked down at the dead man, and into her mind there flowed a river of jagged Old Testament texts which he might have employed to suit the occasion. She yearned to strike a blow for England, to smite the Amalekites, the Philistines, the Midianites. Yet even as the hot wave of fervour swept over her she pulled herself up with scorn of herself for daydreaming. Here she was alone in the Central African forest, alone with a dead man. There was no possible chance of her achieving anything.

It was at this very moment that Rose looked out across the verandah of the bungalow and saw Opportunity peering cautiously at her from the edge of the clearing. She did not recognise it as Opportunity; she had no idea that the man who had appeared there would be the instrument she would employ to strike her blow for England. All she recognised at the moment was that it was Allnutt, the cockney engineer employed by the Belgian gold mining company two hundred miles up the river — a man her brother had been inclined to set his face sternly against as an unchristian example.

But it was an English face, and a friendly one, and the sight of it made her more appreciative of the horrors of solitude in the forest. She hurried onto the verandah and waved a welcome to Allnutt.

Chapter 2

ALLNUTT was still apprehensive. He looked round him cautiously as he picked his way through the native gardens towards her.

"Where's everybody, Miss?" he asked as he came up to her.

"They've all gone," said Rose.

"Where's the Reverend — your brother?"

"He's in there — . He's dead," said Rose.

Her lips began to tremble a little as they stood there in the blazing sunlight, but she would not allow herself to show weakness. She shut her mouth like a trap into its usual hard line.

"Dead, is 'e? That's bad, Miss," said Allnutt — but it was clear that for the moment his sympathy was purely perfunctory. Allnutt's apprehension was such that he could only think about one subject at a time. He had to go on asking questions.

" 'Ave the Germans been 'ere, Miss?" he asked.

"Yes," said Rose. "Look."

The wave of her hand indicated the bare central circle of the village. Had it not been for Von Hanneken, this would have been thronged with a native market, full of chattering, smiling Negroes with chickens and eggs and a hundred other things for barter, and there would have been naked, pot-bellied children running about, and a few cows in sight, and women working in the gardens, and perhaps a group of men coming up from the direction of the river laden with fish. As it was there was nothing, only the bare earth and the ring of deserted huts, and the silent forest hemming them in.

"It's like 'ell, isn't it, Miss?" said Allnutt. "Up at the mine I found it just the sime when I got back from Limbasi. Clean sweep of everything. What they've done with the Belgians, God only knows. And God 'elp 'em, too. I wouldn't like to be a prisoner in the forest of that long chap with the glass eye — 'Anneken's 'is nime, isn't it, Miss? Not a thing stirring at the mine until a nigger who'd esciped showed up. My niggers just bolted for the woods when they 'eard the news. Don't know if they were afride of me or the Germans. Just skipped in the night and left me with the launch."

"The launch?" said Rose, sharply.

"Yerss, Miss. The *African Queen*. I'd been up the river to Limbasi with the launch for stores. Up there they'd 'eard about this war, but they didn't think Von 'Anneken would fight. Just 'anded the stuff over to me and let me go agine. I fort all the time it wouldn't be as easy as they said. Bet they're sorry now. Bet Von 'Anneken done the sime to them as 'e done at the mine. But 'e 'asn't got the launch, nor yet what's in 'er, which 'e'd be glad to 'ave, I daresay."

"And what's that?" demanded Rose.

"Blasting gelatine, Miss. Eight boxes of it. An' tinned grub. An' cylinders of oxygen and hydrogen for that weldin' job on the crusher. 'Eaps of things. Old Von 'Anneken'd find a use for it all. Trust 'im for that."

They were inside the bungalow now, and Allnutt took off his battered sun hat as he realised he was in the presence of death. He bowed his head and lapsed into unintelligibility. Garrulous as he might be when talking of war or of his own experiences, he was a poor hand at formal condolences. But there was one obvious thing to say.

" 'Scuse me, Miss, but 'ow long 'as 'e been dead?"

"He died this morning," said Rose. The same thought came into her mind as was already in Allnutt's. In the tropics a dead man must be buried within six hours, and Allnutt was further obsessed with his desire to get away quickly, to retire again to his sanctuary in the river backwaters far from German observation.

"I'll bury 'im, Miss," said Allnutt. "Don't you worry yourself, Miss. I'll do it all right. I know some of the service. I've 'eard it often enough."

Rose pulled herself together.

"I have my prayer book here. I can read the service," she said, keeping her voice from trembling.

Allnutt came out on the verandah again. His shifty gaze swept the edge of the forest for Germans, before it was directed upon the clearing to find a site for a grave.

"Just there'd be the best place," he said. "The ground'll be light there and 'e'd like to be in the shide, I expect. Where can I find a spide, Miss?"

The pressing importance of outside affairs was of such magnitude in Allnutt's mind that he could not help but say, in the midst of the grisly business —

"We'd better be quick, Miss, in case the Germans come back agine."

And when it was all over and Rose stood in sorrow beside the grave with its makeshift cross, Allnutt moved restlessly beside her.

"Come on darn to the river, Miss," he urged. "Let's get awye from 'ere."

Down through the forest towards the river ran a steep path; where it reached the marshy flats it degenerated into something worse than a track. Sometimes they were up to their knees in mud. They slipped and staggered, sweating under the scanty load of Rose's possessions. Sometimes tree roots gave them momentary foothold. At every step the rank marigold smell of the river grew stronger in their nostrils. Then they emerged from the dense vegetation into blinding sunlight again. The launch swung at anchor, bow upstream, close to the water's edge. The rushing brown water made a noisy ripple round anchor chain and bows.

"Careful now, Miss," said Allnutt. "Put your feet on that stump. That's right."

Rose sat in the launch which was to be so terribly important to her, and looked about her. The launch hardly seemed worthy of her grandiloquent name of *African Queen*. She was squat, flat-bottomed, and thirty feet long. Her paint was peeling off her, and she reeked of decay. A tattered awning roofed in six feet of the stern; amidships stood the engine and boiler, with the stumpy funnel reaching up just higher than the awning. Rose could feel the heat from the thing where she sat, as an addition to the heat of the sun.

"Excuse me, Miss," said Allnutt. He knelt in the bottom of the boat and addressed himself to the engine. He hauled out a panful of hot ashes and dumped them overside with a sizzle and a splutter. He filled the furnace with fresh wood from the pile beside him, and soon smoke appeared from the funnel, and Rose could hear the roar of the draught. The engine began to sigh and splutter — Rose was later to come to know this sequence of sounds so well — and then began to leak grey pencils of steam. In fact, the most noticeable point about the appearance of the engine was the presence of those leaks of steam, which poured out from it here, there, and everywhere. Allnutt peered at his gauges, thrust some more wood into the furnace, and then leaped forward round the engine. With grunts and heaves at the small windlass, he proceeded to haul in the anchor, the sweat pouring from him in rivers. As the anchor came clear, and the rushing current began to sweep the boat in to the bank, he dashed back again to the engine. There was a clanking noise, and Rose felt the propeller begin to vibrate beneath her. Allnutt thrust mightily at the muddy bank with a long pole, snatched the latter on board again, and then came rushing aft to the tiller.

"Excuse me, Miss," said Allnutt again. He swept her aside unceremoniously as he put the tiller over just in time to save the boat from running into the bank. They headed, grinding and clattering, out into the racing brown water.

"I fort, Miss," said Allnutt, " 'ow we might find somewhere quiet be'ind a island, where we couldn't be seen. Then we could talk about what we could do."

"I should think that would be best," said Rose.

The river Ulanga at this point of its course has a rather indefinite channel. It loops and it winds, and its banks are marshy, and it is studded with islands — so frequent indeed are the islands that in some reaches the river appears to be more like a score of different channels, winding their way tortuously through clumps of vegetation. The *African Queen* churned her slow way against the current, quartering across the broad arm in which they had started. Half a mile up on the other bank half a dozen channels offered themselves, and Allnutt swung the boat's nose towards the midmost of them.

"Would you mind 'olding this tiller, Miss, just as it is now?" asked Allnutt.

Rose silently took hold of the iron rod; it was so hot that it seemed to burn her hand. She held it resolutely, with almost a thrill at feeling the *African Queen* waver obediently in her course as she shifted the tiller ever so little. Allnutt was violently active once more. He had pulled open the furnace door and thrust in a few more sticks of fuel, and then he scrambled up into the bows and stood balanced on the cargo, peering up the channel for snags and shoals.

"Port a little, Miss," he called. "Pull it over this side, I mean. That's it! Steady!"

The boat crawled up into a narrow tunnel formed by the meeting of the foliage overhead. Allnutt came leaping back over the cargo and shut off the engine, so that the propeller ceased to vibrate. Then he dashed into the bows once more, and just as the trees at Rose's side began apparently to move forward again as the current overcame the boat's way, he let go the anchor with a crash and rattle, and almost without a jerk the *African Queen* came to a standstill in the green-lighted channel. As the noise of the anchor chain died away a great silence seemed to close in upon them, the silence of a tropical river at noon. There was only to be heard the rush and gurgle of the water, and the sighing and spluttering of the engine. The green coolness might almost have been paradise. And then with a rush came the insects from the island thickets. They came in clouds, stinging mercilessly.

Allnutt came back into the sternsheets. A cigarette hung from his upper lip; Rose had not the faintest idea when he had lighted it, but that dangling cigarette was the finishing touch to Allnutt's portrait. Without it he looked incomplete. Never could Rose picture little Allnutt to herself without a cigarette — generally allowed to

go out — stuck to his upper lip halfway between the centre and the left corner of his mouth. A thin straggling
beard, only a few score black hairs in all, was beginning
to sprout on his lean cheeks. He still seemed restless and
unnerved, as he battled with the flies, but now that they
were away from the dangerous mainland he was better
able to master his jumpiness, or at least to attempt to conceal it under an appearance of jocularity.

"Well, 'ere we are, Miss," he said. "Safe. *And* sound,
as you might say. The question is, wot next?"

Rose was slow of speech and of decision. She remained silent while Allnutt's nervousness betrayed itself
in further volubility.

"We've got 'eaps of grub 'ere, Miss, so we're all right
as far as that goes. Two thousand fags. Two cases of gin.
We can stay 'ere for months, if we want to. Question is,
do we? 'Ow long d'you fink this war'll last, Miss?"

Rose could only look at him in silence. The implica-
tion of his speech was obvious — he was suggesting that
they should remain here in this marshy backwater until
the war should be over, and they could emerge in safety.
And it was equally obvious that he thought it easily the
best thing to do, provided that their stores were sufficient. He had not the remotest idea of striking a blow for
England. Rose's astonishment kept her from replying,
and allowed free rein to Allnutt's garrulity.

"Trouble is," said Allnutt, "we don't know which way
'elp'll come. I s'pose they're going to fight. Old Von 'Anneken doesn't seem to be in two minds about it, does 'e?

If our lot comes from the sea they'd fight their way up the railway to Limbasi, I s'pose. But that wouldn't be much 'elp, when all is said an' done. If they was to, though, we could stay 'ere an' just go up to Limbasi when the time came. I don't know that wouldn't be best, after all. Course, they might come down from British East. They'd stand a better chance of catching Von 'Anneken that way, although 'unting for 'im in the forest won't be no child's play. But if they do that, we'll 'ave 'im between us an' them all the time. Same if they come from Rhodesia or Portuguese East. We're in a bit of a fix whichever way you look at it, Miss."

Allnutt's native cockney wit combined with his knowledge of the country enabled him to expatiate with fluency on the strategical situation. At that very moment, sweating generals were racking their brains over appreciations very similar — although differently worded — drawn up for them by their staffs. An invasion of German Central Africa in the face of a well-led enemy was an operation not lightly to be contemplated.

"One thing's sure, anyway, Miss. They won't come up from the Congo side. Not even if the Belgians want to. There's only one way to come that way, and that's across the lake. And nothing won't cross the lake while the *Louisa*'s there."

"That's true enough," agreed Rose.

The *Königin Luise,* whose name Allnutt characteristically anglicised to *Louisa,* was the police steamer which the German government maintained on the lake. Rose remembered when she had been brought up from the coast, overland, in sections, eight years before. The country had been swept for bearers and workmen then as now, for there had been roads to hack through the forest, and enormous burdens to be carried. The *Königin Luise's* boiler needed to be transported in one piece, and every furlong of its transport had cost the life of a man in the forest. Once she had been assembled and launched, however, she had swept the lake free immediately from the canoe pirates who had infested its waters from time immemorial. With her ten-knot speed she could run down any canoe fleet, and with her six-pounder gun she could shell any pirate village into submission, so that commerce had begun to develop on the lake, and agriculture had begun to spread along such of its shores as were not marshy, and the *Königin Luise,* turning for the moment her sword into a ploughshare, had carried on such an efficient mail and passenger service across the lake that the greater part of German Central Africa was now more accessible from the Atlantic coast, across the whole width of the Belgian Congo, than from the Indian Ocean.

Yet, it was a very significant lesson in sea power that the bare mention of the name of the *Königin Luise* was sufficient to convince two people with a wide experience of the country, like Rose and Allnutt, of the impregnability of German Central Africa on the side of the Congo. No invasion whatever could be pushed across the lake in the face of a hundred-ton steamer with a six-pounder popgun. Germany ruled the waters of the lake as indisputably as England ruled those of the Straits of Dover, and the advantage to Germany which could be derived from this localized sea power was instantly obvious to the two in the launch.

"If it wasn't for the *Louisa*," said Allnutt, "there wouldn't be no trouble here. Old Von 'Anneken couldn't last a month if they could get at him across the Lake. But as it is —"

Allnutt's gesture indicated that, screened on the other three sides by the forest, Von Hanneken might prolong his resistance indefinitely. Allnutt tapped his cigarette with his finger, so that the ash fell down on his dirty white coat. That saved the trouble of detaching the cigarette from his lip.

"But all this doesn't get us any nearer 'ome, does it, Miss? But b-bless me if I can fink what we can do."

"We must do something for England," said Rose instantly. She would have said "We must do our bit," if she had been acquainted with the wartime slang which was at that moment beginning to circulate in England. But what she said meant the same thing, and it did not sound too melodramatic in the African forest.

"Coo!" said Allnutt.

His notion had been to put the maximum possible distance between himself and the struggle; he had taken it for granted that this war, like other wars, should be fought by the people paid and trained for the purpose. Out of touch with the patriotic fervour of the press, nothing had been farther from his thoughts than that he

should interfere. Even his travels, which had necessarily
been extensive, had not increased his patriotism beyond
the point to which it had been brought by the waving of a
penny Union Jack on Empire Day at his board school;
perhaps they had even diminished it — it would be tact-
less to ask by what road and for what reasons an En-
glishman came to be acting as a mechanic-of-all-work on
a Belgian concession in a German colony; it was not the
sort of question anyone asked, not even missionaries nor
their sisters.

"Coo!" said Allnutt again. There was something in-
fectious, something inspiring, about the notion of "doing
something for England."

But after a moment's excitement Allnutt put the allur-
ing vision aside. He was a man of machinery, a man of
facts, not of fancies. It was the sort of thing a kid might
think of, and when you came to look into it there was
nothing really there. Yet, having regard to the light which
shone in Rose's face, it might be as well to temporize, just
to humour her.

"Yerss, Miss," he said, "if there was anyfink we *could*
do I'd be the first to say we ought ter. What's your notion,
specially?"

He dropped the question carelessly enough, secure in
his certainty that there was nothing she could suggest —
nothing, anyway, which could stand against argument.
And it seemed as if he were right. Rose put her big chin
into her hand and pulled at it. Two vertical lines showed
between her thick eyebrows as she tried to think. It

seemed absurd that there was nothing two people with a boat full of high explosive could do to an enemy in whose midst they found themselves, and yet so it appeared. Rose sought in her mind for what little she knew about war.

Of the Russian-Japanese war all she could remember was that the Japanese were very brave men with a habit of shouting "Banzai!" The Boer war had been different — she was twenty then, just when Samuel had entered the ministry, and she could remember that khaki had been a fashionable colour, and that people wore buttons bearing generals' portraits, and that the Queen had sent packets of chocolate to the men at the front. She had read the newspapers occasionally at that time — it was excusable for a girl of twenty to do that in a national crisis.

Then after the Black Week, and after Roberts had gained the inevitable victories, and entered Pretoria, and come home in triumph, there had still been years of fighting. Someone called De Wet had been "elusive" — no one had ever mentioned him without using that adjective. He used to charge down on the railways and blow them up.

Rose sat up with a jerk, thinking at first that the inspiration had come. But next moment the hope faded. There was a railway, it was true, but it ran from a sea which was dominated by England to the head of navigation on the Ulanga at Limbasi. It would be of small use to the Germans now, and to reach any bridge along it she and Allnutt would have to go upstream to Limbasi, which might still be in German hands, and then strike out overland, carrying their explosives with them, with the probability of capture at any moment. Rose had made enough forest journeys to realize the impossibility of the task, and her economical soul was pained at the thought of running a risk of that sort for a highly problematical advantage. Allnutt saw the struggle on her face.

"It's a bit of a teaser, isn't it, Miss?" he said.

It was then that Rose saw the light.

"Allnutt," she said. "This river, the Ulanga, runs into the lake, doesn't it?"

The question was a disquieting one.

"Well, Miss, it does. But if you was thinking of going to the lake in this launch — well, you needn't think about it any more. We can't, and that's certain."

"Why not?"'

"Rapids, Miss. Rocks an' cataracts an' gorges. You 'aven't been there, Miss. I 'ave. There's a nundred miles of rapids down there. Why, the river's got a different nime where it comes out in the lake to what it's called up 'ere. It's the Bora down there. That just shows you. No one knew they was the same river until that chap Spengler —"

"He got down it. I remember."

"Yerss, Miss. In a dugout canoe. 'E 'ad half a dozen Swahili paddlers. Map making, 'e was. There's places where this 'ole river isn't more than twenty yards wide, an' the water goes shooting down there like — like out of a tap, Miss. Canoe might be all right there, but we couldn't never get this ole launch through."

"Then how did the launch get here, in the first place?"

"By rile, Miss, I suppose, like all the other 'eavy stuff.

'Spect they sent 'er up to Limbasi from the coast in sections, and put 'er together on the bank. Why, they *carried*
the *Louisa* to the lake, by 'and, Miss."

"Yes, I remember."

Samuel had nearly got himself expelled from the
colony because of the vehement protests he had made on
behalf of the natives on that occasion. Now her brother
was dead, and he had been the best man on earth.

Rose had been accustomed all her life to follow the
guidance of another — her father, her mother, or her
brother. She had stood stoutly by her brother's side during his endless bickerings with the German authorities.
She had been his appreciative if uncomprehending audi-
ence when he had seen fit to discuss doctrine with her. For
his sake she had slaved — rather ineffectively — to learn
Swahili, and German, and the other languages, thereby
suffering her share of the punishment which mankind had
to bear (so Samuel assured her) for the sin committed at
Babel. She would have been horrified if anyone had told
her that if her brother had elected to be a papist or an infidel she would have been the same, but it was perfectly
true. Rose came of a stratum of society and of history in
which woman adhered to her menfolk's opinions. She was
thinking for herself now for the first time in her life, if ex-
ception can be made of housekeeping problems.

It was not easy, this forming of her own judgments;
especially when it involved making an estimate of a man's
character and veracity. She stared fixedly at Allnutt's face,
through the cloud of flies that hovered round it, and All-

nutt, conscious of her scrutiny, fidgeted uncomfortably. Resolve was hardening in Rose's heart.

Ten years ago she had come out here, sailing with her brother in the cheap and nasty Italian cargo boat in which the Argyll Society had secured passages for them. The first officer of that ship had been an ingratiating Italian, and not even Rose's frozen spinsterhood had sufficed to keep him away. Her figure at twenty-three had displayed the promise which now at thirty-three it had fulfilled. The first officer had been unable to keep his eyes from its solid curves, and she was the only woman on board — in fact, for long intervals she was the only woman within a hundred miles — and he could no more stop himself from wooing her than he could stop breathing. He was the sort of man who would make love to a brass idol, if nothing better presented itself.

It was a queer wooing, and one which had never progressed even as far as a hand clasp — Rose had not even known that she was being made up to. But one of the manœuvres which the Italian had adopted with which to ingratiate himself had been ingenious. At Gibraltar, at Malta, at Alexandria, at Port Said, he had spoken eloquently in his fascinating broken English, about the far flung British Empire; he had called her attention to the big ships, grimly beautiful, and the white ensign fluttering at the stern, and he had spoken of it as the flag upon which the sun never sets. It had been a subtle method of flattery, and one deserving of more success than the unfortunate Italian actually achieved.

It had caught Rose's imagination for the moment, the sight of the rigid line of the Mediterranean squadron battling its way into Valetta harbour through the high steep seas of a levanter with the red-crossed Admiral's flag in the van, and the thought of the wide empire that squadron guarded, and all the glamour and romance of Imperial dominion.

For ten years those thoughts had been suppressed out of loyalty to her brother, who was a man of peace, and saw no beauty in Empire, nor object in spending money on battleships while there remained poor to be fed and heathen to be converted. Now, with her brother dead, the thoughts surged up once more. The war he had said would never come had come at last, and had killed him with its coming. The Empire was in danger. As Rose sat sweating in the sternsheets of the *African Queen,* she felt within her a boiling flood of patriotism. Her hands clasped and unclasped; there was a flush of pink showing through the sallow sunburn of her cheeks.

Restlessly, she rose from her seat and went forward, sidling past the engine, to where the stores were heaped up gunwale-high in the bows — all the miscellany of stuff comprised in the regular fortnight's consignment to the half-dozen white men at the Belgian mine. She looked at it for inspiration, just as she had looked at the contents of the larder for inspiration when confronted with a house-keeping problem. Allnutt came and stood beside her.

"What are those boxes with the red lines on them?" she demanded.

"That's the blasting gelatine I told you about, Miss."

"Isn't it dangerous?"

"Coo, bless you, Miss, no." Allnutt was glad of the opportunity to display his indifference in the presence of this woman who was growing peremptory and uppish. "This is safety stuff, this is. It's quite 'appy in its cases 'ere. You can let it get wet an' it doesn't do no 'arm. If you set fire to it, it just burns. You can 'it it wiv a 'ammer an' it won't go off — at least, I don't fink it will. What you mustn't do is to bang off detonators, gunpowder, like, or cartridges, into it. But we won't be doing that, Miss. I'll put it over the side if it worries you, though."

"No!" said Rose, sharply. "We may want it."

Even if there were no bridges to blow up, there ought to be a satisfactory employment to be found in wartime for a couple of hundredweight of explosive — and lingering in Rose's mind, despite Allnutt's decisive statement that the descent of the river was impossible, there were still the beginnings of a plan, even though it was a vague plan.

In the very bottom of the boat, half covered with boxes, lay two large iron tubes, rounded at one end, conical at the other, and in the conical ends were brass fittings — taps and pressure gauges.

"What are those?" asked Rose.

"They're the cylinders of oxygen and hydrogen. We couldn't find no use for them, Miss, not anyhow. First time we shift cargo I'll drop 'em over."

"No, I shouldn't do that," said Rose. All sorts of incredibly vague memories were stirring in her mind. She looked at the long black cylinders again.

"They look like — like torpedoes," she said at length, musingly, and with the words her plan began to develop apace. She turned upon the cockney mechanic.

"Allnutt," she demanded. "Could you make a torpedo?"

Allnutt smiled pityingly at that.

"Could I mike a torpedo?" he said. "Could I mike —? Arst me to build you a dreadnought, and do the thing in style. You don't really know what you're saying, Miss. It's this way, you see, Miss. A torpedo —"

Allnutt's little lecture on the nature of torpedoes was in the main correct, and his estimate of his incapacity to make one was absolutely correct. Torpedoes are representative of the last refinements of human ingenuity. They cost at least a thousand pounds apiece. The inventive power of a large body of men, picked under a rigorous system of selection, has been devoted for thirty years to perfecting this method of destroying what thousands of other inventors had helped to construct. To make a torpedo capable of running true, in a straight line and at a uniform depth, as Allnutt pointed out, would call for a workshop full of skilled mechanics, supplied with accurate tools, and working under the direction of a specialist in the subject. No one could expect that Allnutt working by himself in the heart of the African forest with only the *African Queen*'s repair outfit could achieve even the veriest botch of an attempt at it. Allnutt fairly let himself go on the allied subjects of gyroscopes, and compressed air chambers, and vertical rudders, and horizontal rudders, and compensating weights. He fairly spouted technicalities. Not even the cockney spirit of enterprise with its willingness to try anything once, which was still alive somewhere deep in Allnutt's interior, could induce him to make the slightest effort at constructing a locomotive torpedo.

Most of the technicalities fell upon deaf ears. Rose heard them without hearing. Inspiration was in full blood.

"But all these things," she said, when at last Allnutt's dissertation on torpedoes came to an end. "All these gyroscopes and things, they're only to make the thing *go,* aren't they?"

"M'm. I suppose so."

"Well," said Rose with decision, at the topmost pinnacle of her inventive phase. "We've got the *African Queen.* If we put this — this blasting gelatine in the front of the boat, with a — what did you say — a detonator there, that would be a torpedo, wouldn't it? Those cylinders. They could stick out over the end, with the gunpowder stuff in them, and the detonators in the tips, where those taps are. Then if we ran the boat against the side of a ship, they'd go off, just like a torpedo."

There was almost admiration mingled with the tolerant pity with which Allnutt regarded Rose now. He had a respect for original ideas, and as far as Allnutt knew this was an original idea. He did not know that the earliest form of torpedo ever used had embodied this invention fifty years ago, although the early users of it took the precaution of attaching the explosive to a spar rigged out ahead of the launch, in this fashion minimizing the danger of the crew's being hoist with its own petard. Allnutt, in fact, made this objection while developing the others which were to come.

"Yerss," he said, "and supposing we did that. Supposing we found something we wanted to torpedo — an' what that would be I dunno, 'cos this is the only boat on this river — and supposing we did torpedo it, what would happen to *us?* It would blow this ole launch and us and everything else all to Kingdom Come. You think again, Miss."

Rose thought, with an unwonted rapidity and lucidity. She was sizing up Allnutt's mental attitude to a nicety. She knew perfectly well what it was she wanted to torpedo. As for going to Kingdom Come, as Allnutt put it with some hint of profanity, she had no objection at all. Rose sincerely believed that if she were to go to heaven she would spend eternity wearing a golden crown and singing perpetual hosannas to a harp accompaniment, and — although this appeared a little strange to her — enjoying herself immensely. And when the question was put to her point-blank by circumstances, she had to admit to herself that it appeared on the face of it that she was more likely to go to heaven than elsewhere. She had followed devoutly her brother's teachings; she had tried to lead a christian life; and, above all, if that life were to end as a result of an effort to help the Empire, the crown and harp would be hers for sure.

But at the same time she knew that no certainty of a

crown and harp would induce Allnutt to risk his life, even if there were the faintest possibility of his end counterbalancing his earlier sins — a matter on which Rose felt uncertainty. To obtain his necessary coöperation she would have to employ guile. She employed it as if she had done nothing else all her life.

"I wasn't thinking," she said, "that we should be in the launch. Couldn't we get everything ready, and have a — what do you call it — a good head of steam up, and then just point the launch towards the ship and send her off? Wouldn't that do?"

Allnutt tried to keep his amusement out of sight. He felt it would be useless to point out to this woman all the flaws in the scheme, the fact that the *African Queen*'s boiler was long past the days when it could take a "good head of steam," and that her propeller, like all single propellers, had a tendency to drive the boat round in a curve so that taking aim would be a matter of chance, and that the *African Queen*'s six knots would be quite insufficient to allow her to approach to take any ship by surprise. There wasn't anything to torpedo, anyway, so nothing could come of this woman's harebrained suggestions. He might as well try to humour her.

"That might work," he said, gravely.

"And these cylinders would do all right for torpedoes?"

"I think so, Miss. They're good an' thick to stand pressure. I could let the gas out of 'em, an' fill 'em up with the gelignite. I could fix up a detonator all right. Revolver cartridge would do."

Allnutt warmed to his subject, his imagination expanding as he let himself go.

"We could cut 'oles in the bows of the launch, and 'ave the cylinders sticking out through them, so as to get the explosion as near the water as possible. Fix 'em down tight wiv battens. It might do the trick, Miss.'"

"All right," said Rose. "We'll go down to the lake and torpedo the *Louisa*."

"Don't talk silly, Miss. You can't do that. Honest you can't. I told you before. We can't get down the river."

"Spengler did."

"In a canoe, Miss, wiv —"

"That just shows we can, too."

Allnutt sighed ostentatiously. He knew perfectly well that there was no possible chance of inducing the *African Queen* to make the descent of the rapids of the Ulanga. He appreciated, in a way Rose could not, the difference between a handy canoe with half a dozen skilled paddlers and a clumsy launch like the *African Queen*. He knew, even if Rose did not, the terrific strength and terrifying appearance of water running at high speed.

Yet, on the other hand Rose represented — constituted, in fact — public opinion. Allnutt might be ready to admit to himself that he was a coward, that he would not lift a hand for England, but he was not ready to tell the world so. Also, although Allnutt had played lone hands occasionally in his life, they were not to his liking. Sooner than plan or work for himself he preferred to be guided — or driven. He was not avid for responsibility. He was glad to hand over leadership to those who desired it, even to the ugly sister of a deceased, despised missionary. He had arrived in Central Africa as a result of his habit of drifting, when all was said and done.

That was one side of the picture. On the other, Rose's scheme appeared to him to be a lunatic's dream. He had not the least belief in their ability to descend the Ulanga, and no greater belief in the possibility of torpedoing the *Königin Luise*. The one part of the scheme which appeared to him to rest on the slightest foundation of reality was that concerned with the making of the torpedoes. He could rely on himself to make detonators capable of going off, and he was quite sure that a couple of gas cylinders full of high explosive would do all the damage one could desire; but as there did not appear the remotest chance of using them he did not allow his thoughts to dwell long on the subject.

What he expected was that after one or two experiences of minor rapids, the sight of a major one might bring the woman to her senses, so that they could settle down in comfortable quiescence and wait — as he wished — for something else to turn up. Failing that, he hoped for an unspectacular and safe shipwreck which would solve the problem for them. Or the extremely unreliable machinery of the *African Queen* might give way irreparably, or even — happy thought — might be induced to do so. And anyway, there were two hundred miles of comfortable river ahead before the rapids began, and Allnutt's temperament was such that anything a week off was hardly worth worrying about.

" 'Ave it yer own wye, then, Miss," he said resignedly. "Only don't blame me. That's all."

He threw his extinct cigarette into the rapid brown water overside and proceeded to take another out of the tin of fifty in the side pocket of his greyish-white jacket. He sat down leisurely beside the engine, cocked his feet up on a pile of wood, and lit the fresh cigarette. He drew in a deep lungful of smoke and expelled it again with satisfaction. Then he allowed the fire in the end to die down towards extinction. The cigarette drooped from his upper lip. His eyelids drooped in sympathy. His wandering gaze strayed to Rose's feet, and from her feet up her white drill frock. He became aware that Rose was still standing opposite him, as if expecting something of him. Startled, he raised his eyes to her face.

"Come on," said Rose. "Aren't we going to start?"

"Wot, *now,* Miss?"

"Yes, now. Come along."

Allnutt was up against hard facts again. It was enough, in his opinion, to have agreed with the lady, to have admitted her to be right, as a gentleman should. Allnutt's impression was that they might start tomorrow if the gods were unkind; next week if they were favourable. To set off like this, at half an hour's notice, to torpedo the German navy seemed to him unseemly, or at least unnatural.

"There isn't two hours of daylight left, Miss," he said, looking down the backwater to the light on the river.

"We can go a long way in two hours," said Rose, shutting her mouth tight. In much the same way, her mother had been accustomed to saying "a penny saved is a penny earned," in the days of the little general shop in the small north country manufacturing town.

"I'll 'ave to get the ole kettle to boil agine," said Allnutt. Yet he got down from his seat and took up his habitual attitude beside the engine.

There were embers still glowing in the furnace; it was only a few minutes after filling it with wood and slamming the door that it began its cheerful roar, and soon after that the engine began to sigh and splutter and leak steam. Allnutt commenced the activities which had been forced upon him by the desertion of his two Negro hands — winding in the anchor, shoving off from the bank, and starting the propeller turning, all as nearly simultaneously as might be. In that atmosphere, where the slightest exertion brought out sweat, these activities caused it to run in streams; his dirty jacket was soaked between his shoulder blades. And, once under way, constant attention at the furnace and the engine gave him no chance to cool down.

Rose watched his movements. She was anxious to learn all about this boat. She took the tiller and set herself to learn to steer. During the first few minutes of the lesson she thought to herself that it was a typical man-made arrangement that the tiller had to be put to the right to turn the boat to the left, but that feeling vanished very quickly; in fact, under Allnutt's coaching, it was not very long before she even began to see sense in a convention which spoke of "port" and "starboard." Rose had always previously had a suspicion that that particular convention had its roots in man's queer taste for ceremonial and fuss.

The voyage began with a bit of navigation which was exciting and interesting, as they threaded their way through backwaters among the islands. There were snags about, and floating vegetation, nearly submerged, which might entangle the screw, and there were shoals and mudbanks to be avoided. It was not until some minutes had elapsed, and they were already a mile or two on their way, that a stretch of easy water gave Rose leisure to think, and she realized with a shock that she had left behind the mission station where she had laboured for ten years, her brother's grave, her home, everything there was in her world, in fact, and all without a thought.

That was the moment when a little wave of emotion almost overcame her. Her eyes were moist and she sniffed a little. She reproached herself with not having been more sentimental about it. Yet immediately after a new surge of feeling overcame the weakness. She thought of the *Königin Luise* flaunting her iron cross flag on the lake where never a white ensign could come to challenge her, and of the Empire needing help, and of her brother's death to avenge. And, womanlike, she remembered the rudenesses and insults to which Samuel had patiently submitted from the officialdom of the colony; they had to be avenged, too. And — although Rose never suspected it — there was within her a lust for adventure, patiently suppressed during her brother's life, and during the monotonous years at the mission. Rose did not realize that she was gratified by the freedom which her brother's death had brought her. She would have been all contrition if she had realized it, but she never did.

As it was, the moment of weakness passed, and she took a firmer grip of the tiller, and peered forward with narrowed eyelids over the glaring surface of the river. Allnutt was being fantastically active with the engine. All those grey pencils of steam oozing from it were indicative of the age of that piece of machinery, and the neglect from which it had suffered. For years the muddy river water had been pumped direct into the boiler, with the result that the water tubes were rotten with rust where they were not plugged with scale.

The water feed pump, naturally, had a habit of choking, and always at important moments, demanding instant attention lest the whole boiler should go to perdition — Allnutt had to work it frantically by hand occasionally, and there were indications that in the past he or his Negro assistants had neglected this precaution, disregarding the doubtful indication of the water gauge, with the result that every water tube joint leaked. Practically every one had been mended at some time or other, in the botched and unsatisfactory manner with which the African climate leads man to be content at unimportant moments; some had been brazed in, but more had been patched with nothing more solid than sheet iron, red lead, and wire.

As a result, a careful watch had to be maintained on

the pressure gauge. In the incredibly distant past, when that engine had been new, a boiler pressure of eighty pounds to the square inch could be maintained, giving the launch a speed of twelve knots. Nowadays, if the pressure mounted above fifteen the engine showed unmistakable signs of dissolution, and no speed greater than four knots could be reached. So Allnutt had the delicate task of keeping the pressure just there, and no higher and no lower, which called for a continuous light diet for the furnace, and a familiarity with the eccentricities of the pressure gauge which could only be acquired by long and continuous study. Nor was this attention to the furnace made any easier by the tendency of the wood fuel to choke the draught with ash — Allnutt, when stoking, had to plan his campaign like a chess player, looking six moves ahead at least, bearing in mind the effect on the draught of emptying the ash pan, the relative inflammability of any one of half a dozen different kinds of wood, the quite noticeable influence of direct sunlight on the boiler, the chances of the safety valve sticking (someone had once dropped something heavy on this, and no amount of subsequent work on it could make it quite reliable again), and the likelihood of his attention being shortly called away to deal with some other crisis.

For the lubrication was in no way automatic nowadays; oil had to be stuffed down the oil cups on the tops of the cylinders, and there were never less than two bearings calling for instant cooling and lubrication, so that Allnutt, when the *African Queen* was under way, was as

active as a squirrel in a cage. It was quite remarkable that
he had been able to bring the launch down single-handed
from the mine to the mission station after the desertion of
his crew, for then he had to steer the boat as well, and
keep the necessary lookout for snags and shoals.

"Wood's running short," said Allnutt, looking up
from his labours, his face grey with grime, and streaked
with sweat. "We'll have to anchor soon."

Rose looked round at where the sun had sunk to the
treetops on the distant bank.

"All right," she said, grudgingly. "We'll find somewhere to spend the night."

They went on, with the engine clanking lugubriously,
to where the river broke up again into a fresh batch of
small waterways. Allnutt cast a last lingering glance over
his engine, and scuttled up into the bows.

"Round 'ere, Miss," he called, with a wave of his arm.

Rose put the tiller over and they surged into a narrow
channel.

"Round 'ere again," said Allnutt. "Steady! There's a
channel 'ere. Bring 'er up into it. Steady! Keep 'er at that!"

They were heading upstream now, in a narrow passage roofed over by trees, whose roots, washed bare by
the rushing brown water, and tangled together almost as
thick as basketwork, constituted the surface of the banks.
Against the sweeping current the *African Queen* made
bare headway. Allnutt let go the anchor and, running
back, shut off steam. The launch swung stationary to her
mooring with hardly a jerk.

For once in a way Rose had been interested in the manœuvres, and she filled with pride at the thought that she had understood them. She didn't usually trouble; when travelling by train she never tried to understand railway signals, and even the Italian first officer had never been able to rouse her interest in ships' work. But today she had understood the significance of it all, of the necessity to moor bows upstream in that narrow fast channel, in consequence of the anchor being in the bows. Rose could not quite imagine what that fast current would do to a boat if it caught it while jammed broadside on across a narrow waterway, but she could hazard a guess that it would be a damaging business. Allnutt stood watching attentively for a moment to make certain that the anchor was not dragging, and then sat down with a sigh in the sternsheets.

"Coo!" he said, "it's 'ot work, ain't it, Miss? I could do a drink."

From the locker beside her he produced a dirty enamel mug, and then a second one.

"Going to 'ave one, Miss?" Allnutt asked.

"No," said Rose, shortly. She knew instinctively that she was about to come into opposition with what Samuel always called Rum. She watched, fascinated. From under the bench on which he sat Allnutt dragged out a wooden case, and from out of the case he brought a bottle, full of some clear liquid like water. He proceeded to pour a liberal portion into the tin mug.

"What is that?" asked Rose.

"Gin, Miss," said Allnutt. "An' there's only river water to drink it with."

Rose's knowledge of strong drink was quite hazy. The first time she had ever sat at a table where it was served had been in the Italian steamer; she remembered the polite amusement of the officers when she and her brother had stiffly refused to drink the purple-red wine which appeared at every meal. During her brother's ministry in England she had heard drink and its evil effects discussed; there were even bad characters in the congregation who were addicted to it, and with whom she had sometimes tried to reason. At the mission, Samuel had striven ineffectively for ten years to persuade his coloured flock to abandon the use of the beer they had been accustomed to brew from time immemorial — Rose knew how very ineffective his arguments had been. And there were festivals when everybody brewed and drank stronger liquors still, and got raging drunk, and made fearful noises, and all had sore heads the next morning; and not even the sore heads had reconciled Samuel to the backsliding of his congregation the night before.

And the few white men all drank, too — although up to this minute Rose, influenced by Samuel's metaphorical description, had been under the impression that their tipple was a fearsome stuff called rum, and not this innocent-appearing gin. Rum, and the formation of unhallowed unions with native women, and the brutal conscription of native labour, had been the triple-headed enemy Samuel was always in arms against. Now, Rose found herself face to face with the first of these sins. Drink made men madmen. Drink rotted their bodies and corrupted their souls. Drink brought ruin in this world and damnation in the next.

Allnutt had filled the other mug overside, and was now decanting water into the gin, trying carefully but not very effectively to prevent too much river alluvium from entering his drink. Rose watched with increasing fascination. She wanted to protest, to appeal to Allnutt's better feelings, even to snatch the terrible thing from him, and yet she stayed inert, unmoving. Possibly it was that commonsense of hers which kept her quiescent. Allnutt drank the frightful stuff and smacked his lips.

"That's better," he said.

He put the mug down. He did not start to be maniacal, nor to sing songs, nor to reel about the boat. Instead, with his sinfulness still wet on his lips, he swung open the gates of paradise for Rose.

"Now I can think about supper," he said. "What about a cup o' tea, Miss?"

Tea! Heat and thirst and fatigue and excitement had done their worst for Rose. She was limp and weary, and her throat ached. The imminent prospect of a cup of tea roused her to trembling excitement. Twelve cups of tea, each, Samuel and she had drunk daily for years. Today she had had none — she had eaten no food either, but at the moment that meant nothing to her. Tea! A cup of tea! Two cups of tea! Half a dozen great mugs of tea, strong, delicious, revivifying! Her mind was suffused with rosy

pictures of an evening's tea drinking, a debauch com-
pared with which the spring sowing festivities at the village by the mission station were only a pale shade.

"I'd like a cup of tea," she said.

"Water's still boiling in the engine," said Allnutt, heaving himself to his feet. "Won't take a minute."

The tinned meat that they ate was reduced, as a result
of the heat, to a greasy semi-liquid mass. The native
bread was dark and unpalatable. But the tea was marvel-
lous. Rose was forced to use sweetened condensed milk
in it, which she hated — at the mission they had cows
until Von Hanneken commandeered them — but not
even that spoilt her enjoyment of the tea. She drank it
strong, mug after mug of it, as she had promised herself,
with never a thought of what it was doing inside her to
the lining of her stomach; probably it was making as
pretty a picture of that as ever she had seen at a Band of
Hope lantern lecture where they exhibited enlarged pho-
tographs of a drunkard's liver. For a moment her body
temperature shot up to fever heat, but presently there
came a blissful perspiration — not the sticky, prickly
sweat in which she moved all day long, but a beneficent
and cooling fluid, bringing with it a feeling of ease and
well-being.

"Those Belgians up at the mine wouldn't never drink
tea," said Allnutt, tilting the condensed milk tin over his
mug of black liquid. "They didn't know what was good."

"Yes," said Rose. She felt positive friendship for Allnutt welling up within her. She slapped at the mosquitoes
without irritation.

When the scanty crockery had been washed and put away, Allnutt stood up and looked about him; the light was just failing.

"Ain't seen no crocodiles in this arm, Miss, 'ave you?" he asked.

"No," said Rose.

"No shallows for 'em 'ere," said Allnutt. "And current's too fast."

He coughed a little self-consciously.

"I want to 'ave a bath before bedtime," he said.

"So do I."

"I'll go up in the bows an' 'ave mine 'olding on to the anchor chain," said Allnutt. "You stay down 'ere and do what you like, Miss. Then if we don't look, it won't matter."

Rose found herself stripping herself naked right out in the open, with a man only a dozen feet away doing the same, and only a slender funnel six inches thick between them. Somehow it did not matter. Rose was conscious that out of the tail of her eye she could see a greyish-white shape lower itself over the launch's bows, and she could hear prodigious kickings and splashings as Allnutt took his bath. She sat naked on the low gunwale in the stern and lowered her legs into the water. The fast current boiled round them, deliciously cool, tugging at her ankles, insidiously luring her further. She slipped over completely, holding on to the boat, trailing her length on the surface of the water. It was like paradise — ever so much better than her evening bath at the mission, in a shallow tin trough of lukewarm water, and obsessed with the continual fear that the unceasing curiosity of the natives might cause prying eyes to be peering at her through some chink or crevice in the walls.

Then she began to pull herself out. It was not easy, what with the pull of the current and the height of the gunwale, but a final effort of her powerful arms drew her up far enough to wriggle at last over the edge. Only then did she realize that she had been quite calmly contemplating calling to Allnutt for assistance, and she felt that she ought to be disgusted with herself, but she could not manage it. She fished a towel out of her tin box of clothes and dried herself, and dressed again. It was almost dark by now, dark enough, anyway, for a firefly on the bank to be visible, and for the noises of the forest to have stilled so much that the sound of the river boiling along the banks seemed to have grown much louder.

"Are you ready, Miss?" called Allnutt, starting to come aft.

"Yes," said Rose.

"You better sleep 'ere in the stern," said Allnutt, "case it rains. I got a couple of rugs 'ere. There ain't no fleas in 'em."

"Where are you going to sleep?"

"For'ard, Miss. I can make a sort of bed out them cases."

"What, on the — the explosives?"

"Yerss, Miss. Won't do it no 'arm."

That was not what had called for the question. To Rose there seemed something against nature in the idea of actually sleeping on a couple of hundredweights of explosive, enough to lay a city in ruins — or to blow in the side of a ship. But she thrust the strangeness of the thought out of her mind; everything was strange now.

"All right," she said, briefly.

"You cover up well," said Allnutt, warningly. "It gets nearly cold on the river towards morning — look at the mist now."

A low white haze was already drifting over the surface of the river.

"All right," said Rose again.

Allnutt retraced his steps into the bows, and Rose made her brief preparations for the night. She did not allow herself to think about the skins — black or white, clean or dirty — which had already been in contact with those rugs. She laid herself on the hard floor boards with the rugs about her and her head on a pillow of her spare clothing. Her mind was like a whirlpool in which circled a mad inconsequence of thoughts. Her brother had died only that morning and it seemed at least a month ago. The memory of his white face was vague although urgent. With her eyes closed, her retinas were haunted with persistent after-images of running water — water foaming round snags, and rippling over shallows, and all agleam with sunshine where the wind played upon it. She thought of the *Königin Luise* queening it on the lake. She thought of Allnutt, only a yard or two from her virgin bed, and of his naked body vanishing over the side of the launch. She thought again of the dead Samuel. The instant resolution which followed to avenge his death caught her on the point of going to sleep. She turned over restlessly. The flies were biting like fiends. She thought of Allnutt's drooping cigarette, and of how she had cheated him into accompanying her. She thought of the play of the light and shade on the water when they had first anchored. And with that shifting pattern in her mind's eye she fell asleep for good, utterly worn out.

Chapter 3

~∞∞∞~

Rose actually contrived to sleep most of the night. It was the rain which woke her up, the rain and the thunder and lightning. It took her a little while to think where she was, lying there in the dark on those terribly hard floor boards. All round her was an inferno of noise. The rain was pouring down as it can only in Central Africa. It was drumming on the awning over her, and streaming in miniature waterfalls from the trees above into the river. The lightning was lighting up brilliantly even this dark backwater, and the thunder roared almost without inter-mission. A warm wind came sweeping along the back-water, blowing the launch upstream a little, so that whenever it dropped for a moment the pull of the current brought her back with a jerk against her moorings like a small earthquake. Almost at once Rose felt the warm rain on her face, blown in by the wind under the awning, and then the awning began to leak, discharging little cataracts of water onto the floor boards round her.

It all seemed to happen at once — one moment she was asleep, and the next she was wet and uncomfortable, and the launch was tugging at her anchor chain. Something moved in the waist of the launch, and the lightning revealed Allnutt crawling towards her, very wet and miserable, dragging his bedding with him. He came pattering up beside her, whimpering, for all the world like a little dog. The leaky awning shot a cataract of water down his neck.

"Coo!" he said, and shifted his position abruptly.

By some kind chance, Rose's position was such that none of these direct streams descended upon her; she was only incommoded by the rain in the wind and the splashes from the floor boards. But that was the only space under the awning as well-protected. Allnutt spent much time moving abruptly here and there, with the pitiless streams searching him out every time. Rose heard his teeth chattering as he came near her, and was for a moment minded to put out her arm and draw him to her like a child; she blushed secretly at discovering such a plan in her mind, for Allnutt was no more a child than she was.

Instead, she sat up and asked —

"What can we do?"

"N-nothing, Miss," said Allnutt, miserably and definitely.

"Can't you shelter anywhere?"

"No, Miss. But this won't last long."

Allnutt spoke with the spiritless patience bred by a lifetime's bad luck. He moved out of one stream of water into another. Samuel, in the same conditions, would have displayed a trace of bad temper — Rose had to measure men by Samuel's standard, because she knew no other man so well.

"You poor man!" said Rose.

"You poor chap" or "You poor old thing" might have sounded more comradely or sympathetic, but Rose had never yet spoken of men as "chaps" or "old things."

"I'm so sorry," said Rose, but Allnutt only shifted uncomfortably again.

Then the storm passed as quickly as it came. In a country where it rains an inch in an hour an annual rainfall of two hundred inches means only two hundred hours' rain a year. For a little while the trees above still tossed and roared in the wind, and then the wind died away, and there was a little light in the backwater, and with the stillness of dawn the sound of the river coursing through the tree roots overshadowed every other noise. The day came with a rush, and for once the sun and the heat were beneficent and life-giving, instead of being malignant tyrants. Rose and Allnutt roused themselves; the whole backwater steamed like a laundry.

"What's to be done before we move on?" asked Rose. It did not occur to her that there was anything they might do instead of moving on. Allnutt scratched at his sprouting beard.

"Got no wood," he said. " 'Ave to fill up with thet. Plenty of dead stuff 'ere, I should fink. An' we'll 'ave to pump out. The ole boat leaks anyways, an' wiv all this rine —"

"Show me how to do that."

So Rose was introduced to the hand pump, which was as old and as inefficient as everything else on board. In theory one stuck the foot of it down between the skin and the floor boards, and then worked a handle up and down, whereupon the water beneath the boards was sucked up and discharged through a spout overside; by inclining the boat over to the side where the pump was, the boat could be got reasonably dry. But that pump made a hard job of it. It choked and refused duty, and squeaked and jammed, and pinched the hands that worked it, all with an ingenuity which seemed quite diabolical. Rose came in the end to hate that pump more bitterly than anything she had ever hated before. Allnutt showed her how to begin the job.

"You go and get the wood," said Rose, settling the pump into the scuppers and preparing to work the handle. "I'll do this by myself."

Allnutt produced an axe which was just as rusty and woebegone as everything else in the boat, hooked the bank with the boat hook, and swung himself ashore with the stern painter in his hand. He vanished into the undergrowth, looking cautiously round at every step for fear of snakes, while Rose toiled away at the pump. There was nothing on earth so ingeniously designed to abolish the feeling of morning freshness. Rose's face empurpled, and the sweat poured down as she toiled away with the cranky thing. At intervals Allnutt appeared on the bank, dumping down fresh discoveries of dead wood to add to the growing pile at the landing place, and then, pulling in on the stern painter, he began the ticklish job of loading the fuel on board, standing swaying perilously on the slippery uneven foothold.

Rose quitted her work at the pump to help him — there was by now only a very little water slopping below the floor boards — and when the wood was all on board, the waist piled high with it, they stopped for breath and looked at each other.

"We had better start now," said Rose.

"Breakfast?" said Allnutt, and then, playing his trump card, "Tea?"

"We'll have that going along," said Rose. "Let's get started now."

Perhaps Rose had all her life been a woman of action and decision, but she had spent all her adult life under the influence of her brother. Samuel had been not merely a man, but a minister, and therefore had a twofold — perhaps fourfold — right to order the doings of his womenfolk. Rose had always been content to follow his advice and abide by his judgment.

But now that she was alone the reaction was violent. She was carrying out a plan of her own devising, and she would allow nothing to stop her, nothing to delay her. She was consumed by a fever for action. That is not to belittle the patriotic fervour which actuated her as well. She was most bitterly determined upon doing something for England; she was so set and rigid in this determination that she never had to think about it, any more than she had to think about breathing, or the beating of her pulse.

She was more conscious of the motive of avenging her brother's death; but perhaps the motive of which she was most conscious was her desire to wipe out the ten years of insults from German officialdom to which the meek Samuel had so mildly submitted. It was the thought of those slights and insults which brought a flush to her cheek and a firmer grip to her hand, and spurred her on to fresh haste.

Allnutt philosophically shrugged his shoulders, much as he had seen his Belgian employers do up at the mine. The woman was a bit mad, but it would be more trouble to argue with her than to obey her, at present; Allnutt was not sufficiently self-analytical to appreciate that most of the troubles of his life resulted from attempts to avoid trouble. He addressed himself, in his usual attitude of prayer, to the task of getting the engine fire going again, and while the boiler was beating he continued the endless task of lubrication. When the boiler began to sigh and gurgle he looked inquiringly at Rose, and received a nod from her. Rose was interested to see how Allnutt proposed to extricate the launch from the narrow channel in which she was moored.

It was a process which called for much activity on Allnutt's part. First he strained at the anchor winch, ineffectively, because the current which was running was too strong to allow him to wind the heavy boat up to the anchor. So he started the screw turning until the *African Queen* was just making headway against the current, and then, rushing forward, he got the anchor clear and wound in. But he did not proceed up the backwater — there was no means of knowing if the way was clear all the way up to the main stream, and some of these backwaters were half a dozen miles long. Instead, he hurried back to the engine, and throttled down until the launch was just being carried down by the current, although the engine was still going ahead.

This gave her a queer contrariwise steerageway, in which one thought in terms of the stern instead of the bow. Allnutt left the engine to look after itself, and hastened back to take the tiller from Rose's hand; he could not trust her with it. He eased the *African Queen* gently down until they reached the junction with the broad channel of the main backwater. Then he scuttled forward and jerked the engine over into reverse, and then, scuttling back to the tiller, he swept the stern round upstream, keeping a wary eye on the bow meanwhile lest the current should push it into the bank, and then, the moment the bow was clear, while catastrophe threatened astern, he dashed forward again, started the screw in the opposite direction, and came leaping back once more to the tiller to hold the boat steady while she gathered way downstream. It was a neat bit of boatmanship; Rose, even with her limited experience, could appreciate it even though some of the implications were lost upon her — the careful balance of eddy against current at the bend, for instance, and the subtle employment of the set of the screw to help in the turn. She nodded and smiled her approval, but Allnutt could not stay for applause. Already there were danger signals from the engine, and Allnutt had to hand over the tiller and resume his work over it.

The *African Queen* resumed her solemn career down the river, with Rose cheerfully directing her. This was the main backwater of the section, a stream a hundred yards wide, so there was no reason to apprehend serious navigational difficulties. Rose had already learned to recognize the ugly V-shaped ripple on the surface caused by a snag just below, and the choppy appearance which indicated shallows, and she understood now the useful point that the *African Queen*'s draught was such that if an underwater danger was so deep as to make no alteration in the appearance of the surface, she could be relied upon to go over it without damage. The main possible source of trouble was in the winds; a brisk breeze whipped the surface of the river into choppy wavelets which obscured the warning signs.

At present today there was no wind blowing. Everything was well. In this backwater, running between marshy uninhabited islands, there was no fear of observation from the shore, the navigation was easy, and the *African Queen*'s engine was in a specially helpful mood, so that she squattered along without any particular crisis arising. Allnutt was even able to snatch half a dozen separate minutes in which to prepare breakfast. He brought Rose's share to her, and she did not even notice the filthy oiliness of his hands. She ate and drank as she held the tiller, and was almost happy.

With a four-knot current to help her the launch slid along between the banks at a flattering speed, and slithered round the bends most fascinatingly. Quite subconsciously Rose was learning things about water in motion, about eddies and swirls, which would be very valuable to her later on.

The heat increased, and as the sun rose higher Rose was no longer able to keep the launch in the shade of the huge trees on the banks. The direct sunlight hit them like a club when they emerged into it, and even back in the sternsheets Rose could feel the devastating heat of the fire and boiler.

She felt sorry for Allnutt, and could sympathize with him over his unhygienic habit of drinking unfiltered river water. At the mission she had seen to it that every drop of water she and Samuel drank was first filtered and then boiled, for fear of hookworm and typhoid and all the other plagues which water can carry. It did not seem to matter now. Under the worn awning she had at least a little shade. Allnutt was labouring in the blazing sun.

Allnutt, as a matter of fact, was one of those men who have become inured to work in impossible temperatures. He had worked as a greaser in merchant ships passing down the Red Sea, in engine rooms at a temperature of a hundred and forty degrees; to him the free air of the Ulanga River was far less stifling, even in the direct sun, than atmospheres with which he was acquainted. It did not occur to him to complain about this part of his life; there was even an æsthetic pleasure to be found in inducing that rotten old engine to keep on moving.

Later the backwater came to an end, merging with the main river again. The banks fell away as they came out on to the broad, stately stream, a full half-mile wide, brilliantly blue in prospect under the cloudless sky, although it still appeared its turbid brown when looked into over the side. Allnutt did not like these open reaches. Von Hanneken, with his army, was somewhere on the banks of the river; perhaps he had outposts watching everywhere. It was only when she was threading her way between islands that the *African Queen* could escape observation. He stood up on the gunwale anxiously, peering at the banks for a sign of a break in them.

Rose was aware of his anxiety and its cause, but she did not share his feelings. She was completely reckless. She did not think it even remotely possible that anything could impede her in the mission she had undertaken. As for being taken prisoner by Von Hanneken, she could not believe such a thing could happen — and naturally she had none of the misgivings which worried Allnutt as to what Von Hanneken would do to them if he caught them obviously planning mischief in the *African Queen*. But she indulged Allnutt in his odd fancy; she swung the *African Queen* round so that she headed across to the far side of the bend, where at the foot of the forest-clad bluffs the head of a long narrow island was to be seen. Rose already knew enough about the river to know that the backwater behind the island was almost for certain the entrance to a fresh chain of minor channels winding between tangled islands and not rejoining the main river for perhaps as much as ten miles.

The *African Queen* clanked solemnly across the river. Her propeller shaft was a trifle out of truth, and numerous contacts with submerged obstructions had bent her propeller blades a little, so that her progress was noisy, and the whole boat shook to the thrust of the screw; but by now Rose was used to the noise and the vibration. It passed unnoticed. Rose stood up and looked forward keenly as they neared the mouth of the backwater. She was quite unconscious of the dramatic picture she presented, sunburned, with set jaw and narrowed eyes, standing at the tiller of the battered old launch in the blinding sunlight. All she was doing was looking out for snags and obstructions.

They glided out of the sunlight into the blessed shade of the narrow channel. The wash of the launch began to break close behind them in greyish-brown waves against the bank; the water plants close to the side began to bow in solemn succession as the boat approached them, lifting their heads again when they were exactly opposite, and then being immediately buried in the dirty foam of the wash. The channel along which they were passing broke into three, and Rose had to exercise quick decision in selecting the one which appeared the most navigable. Then there were periods of anxiety when the channel narrowed and the current quickened, and it seemed possible that they might not get through after all, and the anxiety would only end when the channel suddenly joined a new channel whose breadth and placidity promised freedom from worry for a space.

Those island backwaters were silent places. Even the birds and the insects seemed to be silent in that steaming heat. There were only the tall trees, and the tangled undergrowth, and the aspiring creeper, and the naked tree roots along the banks. It seemed as if the *African Queen*'s clanking progress was the first sound ever to be heard there, and when that sound was stilled, when they anchored to collect more fuel, Rose found herself speaking in whispers until she shook off the crushing influence of the silence.

That first day was typical of all the days they spent descending the river before they reached the rapids. There were incidents, of course. There were times when the backwater they were navigating proved to be jammed by a tangle of tree trunks, and they had to go back cautiously in reverse until they found another channel. There was one occasion when their channel broadened out into a wide, almost stagnant lake surrounded by marshy islands, and full of lilies and weeds that twined themselves round the propeller and actually brought the boat to a standstill, so that Allnutt had to strip himself half naked and lower himself into the water and hack the screw clear with a knife, and then pole the launch out again. Every push of the pole against the loose mud of the bottom brought forth volleys of bubbles from the rotting vegetation, so that the place stank in the sunlight.

It might have been that incident which caused the subsequent trouble with the propeller thrust block, which held them up for half a day while Allnutt laboured over it.

There were times now and then during the day when the heavens opened and cataracts of rain poured down — rain so heavy as to set the floor boards awash,

and to cause Rose to toil long and painfully with that malignant bit of apparatus, the hand pump. They had to expect rain now, for it was the time of the autumn rains.
Rose was only thankful that it was not springtime, for
during the spring rains the storms were much longer and
heavier than those they had to endure now. These little
daily thunderstorms were a mere nothing.

Rose was really alive for the first time in her life. She
was not aware of it in her mind, although her body told
her so when she stopped to listen. She had passed ten
years in Central Africa, but she had not lived during
those ten years. That mission station had been a dreary
place. Rose had not read books of adventure which might
have told her what an adventurous place tropical Africa
was. Samuel was not an adventurous person — he had
not even taken a missionary's interest in botany or philol-
ogy or entomology. He had tried drearily yet persistently
to convert the heathen, without enough success to maintain dinner table conversation over so long a time as ten
years. It had been his one interest in life (small wonder
that Von Hanneken's sweeping requisitions had broken
his heart), and it had therefore been Rose's one interest — and a woefully small one at that.

Housekeeping in a Central African village was a far
duller business than housekeeping in a busy provincial
town, and German Central Africa was the dullest colony
of all Africa. There was only a tiny sprinkling of white
men, and the Kaiser's imperial mandate ran only in the
fringes of the country — in patches along the coast, along
the border of the lake, about the headwaters of the

Ulanga where the gold mine was, and along the railway from the Swahili coast. Save for a very few officials, who conducted themselves towards the missionaries as soldiers and officials might be expected to act towards mere civilians of no standing and aliens to boot, Rose had seen no white men besides Allnutt — he, by arrangement with the Belgian company, used to bring down their monthly consignments of stores and mail from Limbasi — and his visits were conditional upon the *African Queen* being fit to travel, and upon there being no work upon the mining machinery demanding his immediate attention.

And Samuel had not allowed Rose even to be interested in Allnutt's visits. The letters that had come had all been for him, always, and Allnutt was a sinner who lived in unhallowed union with a Negress up at the mine. They had to give him food and hospitality when he came, and to bring into the family prayers a mention of their wish for his redemption, but that was all. Those ten years had been a period of heat-ridden monotony.

It was different enough now. There was the broad scheme of proceeding to the lake and freeing it from the mastery of the Germans; that in itself was enough to keep anyone happy. And for detail to fill in the day there was the river, wide, mutable, always different. There could be no monotony on a river, with its snags and mud bars, its bends and its backwaters, its eddies and its swirls. Perhaps those few days of active happiness were sufficient recompense to Rose for thirty-three years of passive misery.

Chapter 4

⚯

THERE came an evening when Allnutt was silent and moody, as though labouring under some secret grievance. Rose noticed his mood, and looked sharply at him once or twice. There was no feeling of companionship this evening as they drank their tea. And when the tea was drunk Allnutt actually got out the gin bottle and poured himself a drink, the second that day, and drank, and filled his cup again, still silent and sulky. He drank again, and the drink seemed to increase his moodiness. Rose watched these proceedings, disconcerted. She realized by instinct that she must do something to maintain the morale of her crew. There was trouble in the wind, and this gloomy silent drinking would only increase it.

"What's the matter, Allnutt?" she asked, gently. She was genuinely concerned about the unhappiness of the little cockney, quite apart from any thought of what bearing it might have upon the success of her enterprise.

Allnutt only drank again, and looked sullenly down at the ragged canvas shoes on his feet. Rose came over nearer to him.

"Tell me," she said gently again, and then Allnutt answered.

"We ain't goin' no further down the river," he said. "We gone far enough. All this rot about goin' to the lake."

Allnutt did not use the word "rot," but although the word he used was quite unfamiliar to Rose she guessed that it meant something like that. Rose was shocked — not at the language, but at the sentiment. She had been ready, she thought, for any surprising declaration by All-nutt, but it had not occurred to her that there was anything like this in his mind.

"Not going any farther?" she said. "Allnutt! Of course we must!"

"No bloody 'of course' about it," said Allnutt.

"I can't think what's the matter," said Rose, with perfect truth.

"The river's the matter, that's what. And Shona."

"Shona!" repeated Rose. At last she had an inkling of what was worrying Allnutt.

"If we go on to-morrer," said Allnutt, "we'll be in the rapids to-morrer night. An' before we get to the rapids we'll 'ave to go past Shona. I'd forgotten about Shona until last night."

"But nothing's going to happen to us at Shona."

"Ain't it? Ain't it? 'Ow do you know? If there's any-wheres on this river the Germans are watching it'll be Shona. That's where the road from the south crosses the river. There was a nigger ferry there before the Germans ever came 'ere. They'll 'ave a gang watching there. Strike-me-dead-certain. An' there ain't no sneaking past Shona. I been there, in this old *African Queen.* I knows what the river's like. It's just one big bend. There ain't no backwaters there, nor nothing. You can see clear across from one side to the other, an' Shona's on a 'ill on the bank."

"But they won't be able to stop us."

"Won't be able —! Don't talk silly, Miss. They'll 'ave rifles. Some of them machine guns, p'raps. Cannons p'raps. The river ain't more than 'alf a mile wide."

"Let's go past at night, then."

"That won't do, neither. 'Cause the rapids start just below Shona. That 'ill Shona stands on is the beginning of the cliffs the river runs between. If we was to go past Shona in the dark we'd 'ave to go on darn the rapids in the dark. An' I ain't goin' darn no rapids in the dark, neither. An' I ain't goin' darn no rapids at all, neither, neither. We didn't ought to 'ave come darn as far as this. It's all dambloody barmy. They might find us 'ere, if they was to come out in a canoe from Shona. I'm goin' back tomorrer up to that other backwater we was in yesterdye. That's the sifest plice for us."

Allnutt had shaken off all shame and false modesty. He preferred appearing a coward in Rose's eyes to risking going under fire at Shona, or to attempting the impossible descent of the gorges of the Ulanga. There was not going to be any more hankypanky about it. He drank neat gin to set the seal on his resolution.

Rose was white with angry disappointment. She tried

to keep her temper, to plead, to cajole, but Allnutt was in no mood for argument. For a while he was silent now, and made no attempt to combat Rose's urgings, merely opposing to them a stolid inertia. Only when, in the growing darkness, Rose called him a liar and a coward — and Rose in her sedate upbringing had never used those words to anyone before — did he reply.

"Coward yerself," he said. "You ain't no lady. No, Miss. That's what my poor ole mother would 'ave said to *you*. If my mother was to 'ear you —"

When a man who is drinking neat gin starts talking about his mother he is past all argument, as Rose began to suspect. She drew herself stiffly together in the stern-sheets while Allnutt's small orgy continued. She was alone in a small boat with a drunken man — a most dreadful situation. She sat tense in the darkness, ready to battle for her life or her virtue, and quite certain that one or the other would be imperiled before morning. Every one of Allnutt's blundering movements in the darkness put her on the qui vive. When Allnutt knocked over his mug or poured himself out another drink she sat with clenched fists, convinced that he was preparing for an assault. There was a frightful period of time, while Allnutt was in muddled fashion reaching beneath the bench for the case of gin to find another bottle, during which she thought he was crawling towards her.

But Allnutt was neither amorous nor violent in his cups. His mention of his mother brought tears into his eyes. He wept at his mother's memory, and then he wept over the fate of Carrie, which was his name for the brawny Swahili-speaking Negress who had been his mistress at the mine, and who was now heaven knew where in the train of Von Hanneken's army. Then he mourned over his own expatriation, and he sobbed through his hiccups at the thought of his boyhood friends in London. He began to sing, with a tunelessness which was almost unbelievable, a song which suited his mood —

"Gimmy regards ter Leicester Square,
Sweet Piccadilly an' Myefair.
Remember me to the folks darn there;
They'll understa-and."

He dragged out the last note to such a length that he forgot what he was singing, and he made two or three unavailing attempts to recapture the first fine careless rapture before he ceased from song. Then in his mutterings he began to discuss the question of sleep, and, sure enough, the sound of his snores came before long through the darkness to Rose's straining ears. She had almost relaxed, when a thump and a clatter from Allnutt's direction brought her up to full tension again. But his peevish exclamations told her that he had only fallen from the seat to the floor boards, mugs, bottle and all, and in two minutes he was happily snoring again, while Rose sat stiff and still, and chewed the cud of her resentment against him, and the reek of the spilt gin filled the night air.

Despair and hatred kept her from sleep. At that moment she had no hope left on earth. Her knowledge of men — which meant her knowledge of Samuel and of her father — told her that when a man said a thing he meant it, and nothing on earth would budge him from that decision. She could not believe that Allnutt would ever be induced or persuaded or bullied into attempting to pass Shona, and she hated him for it. It was the first time she had ever really set her heart on anything, and Allnutt stood in her way, immovable. Rose wasted no idle dreams on Quixotic plans of getting rid of Allnutt and conducting the *African Queen* single-handed; she was level-headed enough and sufficiently aware of her own limitations not to think of that for a second.

At the same time she seethed with revolt and resentment, even against the godlike male. Although for thirty years she had submitted quite naturally to the arbitrary decisions of the superior sex, this occasion was different. She wanted most passionately to go on; she knew she ought to; conscience and inclination combined to make her resent Allnutt's change of front. There was nothing left to live for, if she could not get the *African Queen* down to the lake to strike her blow for England; and such was the obvious sanctity of such a mission that she stood convicted in her own mind of mortal sin if she did not achieve it. Her bitterness against Allnutt increased.

She resolved, as the night wore on, to make Allnutt pay for his arbitrariness. She set her teeth, she chewed at her nails — and Rose's mother's slipper had cured her of nail-biting at the age of twelve — as she swore to herself to make Allnutt's life hell for him. Rose had never tried to raise hell in her life, but in her passion of resentment she felt inspired to it. In the darkness her jaw came forward, and her lips compressed until her mouth was no more than a thin line, and there were deep parentheses from her nostrils to the corners of her mouth. Anyone who could have seen Rose at that moment would have taken her for a shrew, a woman with the temper of a fiend. Now that Samuel was dead, Rose had no use for patience or resignation or charity or forgiveness or any of the passive Christian virtues.

Nor was her temper improved by a night of discomfort. Cramps and aches made her change her position, but she could not, even if she would, lie down in the sternsheets where Allnutt was all asprawl across the boat, and she would not make her way forward to take up All-nutt's usual nest among the explosives. She sat and suffered on the ribbed bench, on which she had sat all day, and even her shapely and well-covered hindquarters protested. She slept, towards morning, by fits and starts, but that amount of sleep did nothing towards mollifying her cold rage.

Dawn revealed to her Allnutt lying like a corpse on the floor boards. His face, hardly veiled by the sprouting beard, was a dirty grey, and from his open mouth came soft but unpleasing sounds. There was no pleasure in the sight of him. Rose got to her feet and stepped over him; she would have spurned him with her foot, save that she did not want to rouse him to violent opposition to what she was going to do. She dragged out the case of gin, took out a bottle and stripped the lead foil from the end. The cork was of the convenient kind which needs no cork-screw. She poured the stuff overside, dropped the bottle in after it, and began on another.

When for the third time the glug-glug-glug of poured liquid reached Allnutt's ears he muttered something, opened his eyes, and tried to sit up.

"Jesus!" he said.

It was not the sight of what Rose was doing which called forth the exclamation, for he still did not know the reason of the noise which had roused him. Allnutt's head was like a lump of red-hot pain. And it felt as if his head, besides, were nailed to the floor boards, so that any attempt at raising it caused him agony. And his eyes could not stand the light; opening them intensified the pain. He shut his eyes and moaned; his mouth was parched and his throat ached, too.

Allnutt was not a natural-born drinker; his wretched frame could not tolerate alcohol. It is possible that his small capacity for liquor played a part in the unknown explanation of his presence in German Central Africa. And one single night's drinking always reduced him to this pitiful state, sick and white and trembling, and ready to swear never to drink again — quite content, in fact, not to drink for a month at least.

Rose paid no attention to his moaning and whimpering. She flung one look of scorn at him and then poured the last bottle of the case overside. She went forward and dragged the second case of gin out from among the boxes of stores. She took Allnutt's favourite screwdriver and began to prize the case open, with vicious wrenches of her powerful wrist. As the deal came away from the nails with a splintering crash, Allnutt rolled over to look at her again. With infinite trouble he got himself into a sitting position, with his hands at his temples, which felt as if they were being battered with white-hot hammers. He looked at her quite uncomprehending with his aching eyes.

"Coo, Jesus!" he said, pitifully.

Rose wasted neither time nor sympathy on him; she went calmly on pouring gin overside. Allnutt got to his knees with his arms on the bench. At the second attempt he got his knees up on the bench, with his body hanging overside. Rose thought he would fall in, but she did not care. He leaned over the gurgling brown water and drank feverishly. Then he slumped back onto the bench and promptly brought up all the water he had drunk, but he felt better, all the same. The light did not hurt his eyes now.

Rose dropped the last bottle into the river, and made certain there was no other in the case. She returned to the sternsheets, passing him close enough to touch him, but apparently without noticing his presence. She took her toilet things from her tin box, picked up a rug, and went back again into the bows. By the time Allnutt was able to turn his head in that direction the rug was pinned across the funnel stay to the funnel, screening her from view.

When she took down the rug again her toilet was obviously finished; she folded the rug, still without paying him the least attention, and began to prepare her breakfast, and then to eat it with perfect composure. Breakfast completed, she cleared all away, and came back into the stern, but she still gave him neither look nor word. With an appearance of complete abstraction she picked out the dirty clothes from her tin box and began to wash them overside, pinning each garment out to dry to the awning overhead. And when she had finished the washing she sat down and did nothing; she did not even look at Allnutt. This was, in fact, the beginning of the great silence.

Rose had been able to think of no better way of making Allnutt's life a hell — she did not realize that it was the most effective way possible. Rose had remembered occasions when Samuel had seen fit to be annoyed with her, and had in consequence withdrawn from her the light of his notice and the charm of his conversation, sometimes for as much as twenty-four hours together. Rose remembered what a dreadful place the bungalow had become then, and how Samuel's silence had wrought upon her nerves, until the blessed moment of forgiveness. She could not hope to equal Samuel's icily impersonal quality, but she would do her best, especially as she could not, anyway, bring herself to speak to the hateful Allnutt. She had no reliance in her ability to nag, and nagging was the only other practicable method of making Allnutt's life hell for him.

During the morning, Allnutt did not take very special

notice of his isolation. His wretched mind and body were too much occupied in getting over the effects of drinking a bottle and a half of overproof spirit in a tropical climate. But as the hours passed, and draught after draught of river water had done much towards restoring their proper rhythm to his physiological processes, he grew restless. He felt that by now he had earned forgiveness for his late carouse; and it irked him unbearably not to be able to talk as much as he was accustomed. He thought Rose was angry with him for his drunkenness; he attached little importance, in his present state, to the matter of his refusal to go on past Shona and down the rapids.

"Coo, ain't it 'ot?" he said. Rose paid him no attention.

"We could do wiv anuvver storm," said Allnutt. "Does get yer cool fer a minute, even if these little b-beggars bite 'arder than ever after it."

Rose remembered a couple of buttons that had to be sewn on. She got out the garment and her housewife, and calmly set about the business. At her first movement Allnutt had thought some notice of his existence was about to be taken, and he felt disappointed when the purpose of the movement became apparent.

"Puttin' yer things to rights prop'ly, ain't yer, Miss?" he said.

A woman sewing has a powerful weapon at her disposition when engaged in a duel with a man. Her bent head enables her to conceal her expression without apparently trying; it is the easiest matter in the world for her to simulate complete absorption in the work in hand when actually she is listening attentively; and if even then she feels disconcerted or needs a moment to think, she can always play for time by reaching for her scissors. And some men — Allnutt was an example — are irritated effectively by the attention paid to trifles of sewing instead of to their fascinating selves.

It took only a few minutes for Allnutt to acknowledge the loss of the first round of the contest.

"Ain't yer goin' to answer me, Miss?" he said, and then, still eliciting no notice, he went on — "I'm sorry for what I done last night. There! I don't mind sayin' it, Miss. What wiv the gin bein' there to my 'and, like, an' the 'eat, an' what not, I couldn't 'elp 'avin' a drop more than I should 'ave. You've pyed me back proper already, pourin' all the rest of it awye, now 'aven't you, Miss? Fair's fair."

Rose made no sign of having heard, although a better psychologist than Allnutt might have made deductions from her manner of twirling the thread round the shank and the decisive way in which she oversewed to end off. Allnutt lost his temper.

" 'Ave it yer own wye, then, yer psalm-singing ole bitch," he said, and pitched his cigarette end overside with disgust, and lurched up into the bows. Rose's heart came up into her mouth at his first movement, for she thought he was about to proceed to physical violence. His true purpose fortunately became apparent before she had time to obey her first impulse and put down her sewing to defend herself. She converted her slight start into a test of the ability of the button to pass through the hole.

From his earliest days, from his slum-bred father and mother, Allnutt had heard, and believed, that the ideal life was one with nothing to do, nothing whatever, and plenty to eat. Yet, up to today, he had never experienced that ideal combination. He had never been put to the necessity of amusing himself; he had always had companions in his leisure periods. Solitude was as distressing to him as responsibility, which was why, when his Negro crew had deserted him at the mine, he had involved himself in considerable personal exertion to come down to the mission station and find Rose and Samuel. And to be cooped, compulsorily, in a thirty-foot boat was harassing to the nerves, especially nerves as jangled as Allnutt's. Allnutt fidgeted about in the bows until he got on Rose's nerves as well; but Rose kept herself under control.

It was not long before Allnutt, moving restlessly about the boat, began to occupy himself with overhauling the engine. For a long time that engine had not had so much attention as Allnutt lavished on it today. It was greased and cleaned and nursemaided, and a couple of the botched joints were botched a little more effectively. Then Allnutt found he was thoroughly dirty, and he washed himself with care, and in the middle of washing he thought of something else, and he went to his locker and got out his razor, and cleansed it of the thick grease which kept it from rusting, and set himself to shave. It was only sheer laziness which had caused him to cease to shave when war broke out, and which accounted for that melodramatic beard. Shaving a beard like that was painful, but Allnutt went through with it, and when it

was over he stroked his baby-smooth cheeks with satisfaction. He put cylinder oil on his tousled hair and
worked at it until he had achieved the ideal coiffure, with
an artistic quiff along his forehead. He replaced his
things in his locker with elaborate care, and sat down to
recover. Five minutes later he was on his feet again, moving about the cramped space, wondering what he could
do now. And all round him was the silence of the river;
that in itself was sufficient to get on his nerves.

Chapter 5

A MAN of stronger will than Allnutt, or a more intelligent one, might have won that duel with Rose. But Allnutt was far too handicapped. He could not do chess problems in his head, or devote his thoughts to wondering what was the military situation in Europe, or debate with himself the pros and cons of Imperial Preference, or piece together all the fragments of Shakespeare he could remember. He knew no fragments of Shakespeare at all, and his mind had never been accustomed to doing any continuous thinking, so that in a situation in which there was nothing to do but think he was helpless. In the end, it was the noise of the river eternally gurgling round the tree roots which broke down his last obstinacy.

Allnutt had made several attempts to get back on a conversational footing with Rose, and only once had he managed to induce her to say anything.

"I hate you," she had said then. "You're a coward and you tell lies, and I won't speak to you ever."

And she had shaken herself free. The very first advance Allnutt had made had surprised her. All she had hoped to achieve was revenge, to make Allnutt suffer for the failure of her scheme. She had not believed it possible that she might reduce him to obedience by this means. She had no idea of the power at her disposal, and she had never had to do with a weak-willed man before. Her brother and her father were men with streaks of flintlike obstinacy within their pulpy exteriors. It was only when Allnutt began to ask for mercy that it dawned upon her that she might be able to coerce him into obeying her. By that time, too, she had a better appreciation of the monotony of the river, and its possible effect on Allnutt.

Her one fear was lest Allnutt should become violent. She had steeled herself to hear unmoved anything he might say to her, or any indelicate expressions he might employ, but the thought of physical force undoubtedly gave her a qualm. But she was a well-set-up woman, and she put unobtrusively into her waistbelt the stiletto from her workbag. If he should try to rape her (Rose did not use the word "rape" to herself; she thought of his trying to "do that to her") she would dig at him with it; its point was sharp.

She need not have worried. Physical violence, even towards a woman, was a long way from Allnutt's thoughts. It might have been different if there had been any gin left to give him the necessary stimulus, but providentially all the gin was in the river.

Just as Rose had underestimated her power, so had

Allnutt underestimated his offence. At first he had taken it for granted that Rose was angry with him because he had got drunk. Her scheme for going on down the river was so ludicrously wild that he hardly thought about it when the silence began; it was only by degrees that he came to realize that Rose was in earnest about it, and that she would give him no word and no look until he agreed to it. It was this realization which stiffened up his obstinacy after his preliminary apologies, and strengthened him to endure another twenty-four hours of torture.

For it was torture, of a refinement only to be imagined by people of Allnutt's temperament who have undergone something like his experiences. There was nothing to do at all, except to listen to the gurgle of the river among the tree roots and to endure the attacks of insects in the crushing heat. Allnutt could hardly even walk about in the cumbered launch. Silence was one of the things he could not endure; his childhood in shrieking streets, and his subsequent life in machine shops and engine rooms, had given him no taste for it. But the silence was only a minor part of the torture; what Allnutt felt more keenly still was Rose's presence, and her manner of ignoring him. That roiled him inexpressibly. It is possible that he could have borne the silence of the river if it had not been for the continuous irksomeness of Rose's silent presence. That hurt him in a sensitive spot, his vanity, in a manner of speaking, or his self-consciousness.

In the end it even interfered with Allnutt's sleep, which was the surest sign of its effectiveness. Insomnia was a quite new phenomenon to Allnutt, and worried him enormously. Days without exercise for either body or mind, a slightly disordered digestion, and highly irritable nerves combined to deprive Allnutt of sleep for one entire night. He shifted and twisted and turned on his uncomfortable bed on the explosives; he sat up and smoked cigarettes; he fidgeted and he tried again, unavailingly. He really thought there was something seriously wrong with him. Then in the morning, faced with yet another appalling blank day, he gave in.

"Let's 'ear wotcha wanter do, Miss," he said. "Tell us, and we'll do it. There, Miss."

"I want to go on down the river," said Rose.

Once more appalling visions swept across Allnutt's imagination, of machine guns and rocks and whirlpools, of death by drowning, of capture by the Germans and death in the forest of disease and exhaustion. He was frightened, and yet he felt he could not stay a minute longer in this backwater. He was panicky with the desire to get away, and in his panic he plunged.

"All right, Miss," he said. "Carm on."

Some time later the *African Queen* steamed out of the backwater into the main river. It was a broad, imposing piece of water here. There was more wind blowing than there had been for some time, and up the length of the river ran long easy waves, two feet high, on which the *African Queen* pitched in realistic fashion, with splashes of spray from the bows sizzling occasionally on the boiler.

Rose sat at the tiller in a fever of content. They were

on their way to help England once more. The monotony of inaction was at an end. The wind and the waves suited her mood. It is even possible that the thought that they were about to run into danger added to her ecstasy.

"That's the 'ill Shona stands on," Allnutt yelled to Rose, gesticulating. Rose only nodded, and Allnutt bent over the fire again, cursing under his breath. Even when they had started Allnutt had still hoped. He had not been quite sure how far down Shona was. Something might easily happen to postpone the issue before they reached there. He really meant to burn out a water tube at the right moment, so that they would have to lie up again for repairs before making the attempt. But now they were in sight of Shona unexpectedly; if the engine were disabled the current would bring them right down to the place, and there was no shelter on either bank. They would be prisoners instantly, and, appalling though the choice was, Allnutt would rather risk his life than be taken prisoner. He began feverishly to nurse the engine into giving its best possible performance.

The waist of the launch was heaped with the wood collected that morning; Allnutt crouched behind the pile and hoped it could stop a bullet. He saw that ready to his hand were the chunks of rotten wood which would give an instant blaze and a quick head of extra steam when the moment came. He peered at the gauges. The *African Queen* came clattering majestically down the river, a feather of smoke from her funnel, spray flying from her bows, a white wake behind her.

The Askaris on the hills saw her coming, and ran to fetch the white commandant of the place. He came hurriedly to the mud walls (Shona is a walled village) and mounted the parapet, staring at the approaching launch through his field glasses. He took them from his eyes with a grunt of satisfaction; he recognized her as the *African Queen,* the only launch on the Ulanga, for which he had received special orders from Von Hanneken to keep a sharp lookout. She had been lost to sight — skulking in backwaters, presumably — for some time, and her capture was desirable. The German captain of reserve was glad to see her coming in like this. Presumably the English missionaries and the mechanic had tired of hiding, or had run short of food, and were coming in to surrender.

There could be no doubt that that was what they intended, for a mile below Shona, just beyond the next bend, in fact, the navigation of the river ceased where it plunged into the gorges. She would be a useful addition to his establishment; he would be able to get about in her far more comfortably than by the forest paths. And if ever the English, coming up by the old caravan route, reached the opposite side of the river, the launch would be of great assistance in the defence of the crossing. The mere mention of her capture would be a welcome change in the eternal dull reports he had to send by runner to Von Hanneken.

He was glad she was coming in. He stood and watched her, a white speck on the broad river. Clearly the people in her did not know where the best landing place was. They were keeping to the outside of the bend in the fast current, on the opposite side to the town. They must be intending to come in below the place, where there was a belt of marshy undergrowth — it was silly of them. When they came in he would send a message to them to come back up the river to the canoe landing place, where he could come and inspect them without getting himself filthy and without having to climb the cliff.

He walked over to the adjacent face of the town to observe her further progress round the bend. The fools were still keeping to the outside of the bend. They showed no signs of coming in at all. He put his hands to his helmet brim, for they were moving now between him and the sun, and the glare was dazzling. They weren't coming in to surrender after all! God knew what they intended, but whatever it was, they must be stopped. He lifted up his voice in a bellow, and his dozen Askaris came trotting up, their cartridge belts over their naked chests, their Martini rifles in their hands. He gave them their orders, and they grinned happily, for they enjoyed firing off cartridges, and it was a pleasure which the stern German discipline denied them for most of their time. They slipped cartridges into the breeches, and snapped up the levers. Some of them lay down to take aim. Some of them kept their feet, and aimed standing up, as their instincts taught them. The sergeant chanted the mystic words, which he did not understand, telling them first to aim and then to fire. It was a ragged enough volley when it came.

The captain of reserve looked through his glasses; the launch showed no signs of wavering from her course, and kept steadily on, although the fools in her must have heard the volley, and some at least of the bullets must have gone somewhere near.

"Again," he growled, and a second volley rang out, and still there was no alteration of course towards the town on the part of the launch. This was growing serious. They were almost below the town now, and approaching the farther bend. He snatched a rifle from one of the Askaris and threw himself on his stomach on the ramparts. Someone gave him a handful of cartridges, and he loaded and took aim. They were right in the eye of the sun now, and the glare off the water made the foresight indistinct. It was very easy to lose sight of the white awning of the boat as he aimed.

A thousand metres was a long range for a Martini rifle with worn rifling. He fired, reloaded, fired again, and again, and again. Still the launch kept steadily on. As he pointed the rifle once more at her something came between him and the launch; it was the trees on the farther point. They were round the corner. With a curse he jumped to his feet and, rifle in hand, ran lumbering along the ramparts with his Askaris behind him. Sweating, he galloped down across the village clearing and up the steep path through the forest on the other side. Climbing until he thought his heart would burst, he broke through the undergrowth at last at the top of the cliff, where he would look down the last reach of the river before the cataract. They had almost reached the farther end; the launch was just swinging round to take the turn. The captain of reserve put his rifle to his shoulder and fired hurriedly, twice, although, panting as he was, there was no chance of hitting. Then they vanished down the gorge, and there was nothing more he could do.

Yet he stood staring down between the cliffs for a long minute. Von Hanneken would be furious at the news of the loss of the launch, but what more could he have done? He could not justly be expected to have foreseen this. No one in his senses would have taken a steam launch into the cataract, and a reserve officer's training does not teach a man to guard against cases of insanity. The poor devils were probably dead already, dashed to pieces against the rocks; and the launch was gone for good and all. He could not even take steps to recover fragments, for the tall cliffs between which the river ran were overhanging and unscalable, and not five kilometres from Shona the country became so broken and dense that the course of the lower Ulanga was the least known, least explored part of German Central Africa. Only Spengler — another born fool — had got through it.

The captain of reserve was not going to try; he formed that resolve as he turned away from the cliff top. And as he walked back to Shona, bathed in sweat, he was still undecided whether he should make any mention of this incident in his report to Von Hanneken. It would only mean trouble if he did; Von Hanneken would be certain it was all his fault, and Von Hanneken was a tyrant. It might be better to keep quiet about it. The launch was gone, and the poor devils in it were dead. That little worm of a missionary and his horse-faced wife — or was it his sister? Sister, of course. And the English mechanic who worked at the Belgian mine. He had a face like a rat. The world would not miss them much. But he was sorry for the poor devils, all the same.

When he came up through the gate again into Shona he was still not sure whether or not he would inform Von Hanneken of the incident. The Askaris would gossip, of course, but it would be a long time before the gossip reached Von Hanneken's ears.

Chapter 6

⸎

THE rivers of Africa are nearly all rendered unnavigable along some part of their courses by waterfalls and cataracts. The rivers on their way to the sea fall from the central table-land into the coastal plain, but the Ulanga is not one of this category. Its course is inland, towards the Great Lakes, and its cataracts mark the edge of the Great Rift Valley. For in the centre of Africa an enormous tract of territory, longer than it is wide, has sunk bodily far below the level of the tableland, forming a deep trough, of a total area approaching that of Europe, in which are found the Great Lakes with their own river system, and, ultimately, the source of the Nile.

Along much of their length the sides of this trough are quite steep, but the Ulanga, as befits the noble river it is, has scoured out of its bed and cut back along it, so that nowhere in its course is there an actual waterfall; its cataracts indicate the situation of strata of harder rock which have not been cut away as efficiently as have the softer beds. The natural result is that in its course from the tableland to the valley the Ulanga flows frequently through deep, sunless gorges between high cliffs; overhead is rough, steep country, untraveled and unmapped, in which the presence of a river could hardly be suspected.

At Shona the river begins its descent; because this is the last point at which the river may be crossed by raft or canoe, the old slave caravan route along the edge of the rift passes the Ulanga here, and Shona grew up as the market at the point of intersection of caravan route and river route. The choice of site at the top of the cliff overlooking the river, where the gorge has actually begun, was of course due to the need of protection from slave raiders, who, being quite willing to sell their own fathers if they saw profit in it, were never averse to snapping up business acquaintances should they be so careless as not to take proper precautions.

It was down the outside of the great bend on which Shona stands that Rose steered the *African Queen.* It was convenient that on this course they not merely kept in the fastest current but also were as far away as possible from the village. She looked up the steep bank, across the wide expanse of water. The forest came to an end halfway up the slope; near the crest she could see high red walls, and above them the thatched roofs of the huts on the very top of the hill. It was too far to see details. She could see no sign of their coming being noticed. There was no sign of life on the banks; and as they went on down the river the banks grew rapidly higher and steeper into nearly vertical walls of rock, fringed at the foot with a precarious growth of vegetation.

She looked at the red walls on the top of the cliff; she thought she could see a movement there, but it was half a mile off and she could not be sure. Perhaps Von Hanneken had swept off the inhabitants here as he had done along the rest of the river, to leave a desert in the possible path of the approach of the English. They were practically opposite the town now, and nothing had happened. A glance at the near bank showed her the speed at which they were moving; the river was already running much faster in its approach to the cataracts.

Suddenly there was a peculiar multiple noise in the air, like bees in a violent hurry accompanied by the sound of tearing paper. Rose's mind had just time to take note of the sound when she heard the straggling reports of the rifles which had caused it. The volley echoed back from cliff to cliff, growing flatter the longer the sound lasted.

"They've got us!" said Allnutt, leaping up in the waist. His face was lopsided with excitement. Rose could pay no attention to him. She was looking keenly ahead at the swirls on the surface. She was keeping the *African Queen* in the fastest water along the very edge of the back eddy off the bank.

There came another volley which still left them untouched. Rose edged the tiller over so as to get more in midstream, in order to take the reverse bend which was rapidly approaching. Allnutt remained standing in the waist; he had forgotten all about taking shelter behind the woodpile. Rose swung the tiller over for the bend; so absorbed was she in her steering that she did not notice the bullet which whipped close by her as she did so. A moment later the whole boat suddenly rang like a harp, and Allnutt turned with a jump. The wire funnel stay on the starboard side had parted close above the gunwale; the long end hung down by the funnel. Even as Allnutt noted it there was a metallic smack, and two holes showed high up in the funnel. Rose had brought the tiller over again, straightening the launch on her course after taking the bend. The next moment Shona vanished behind the point, and Allnutt stood shaking his fists in derision at the invisible enemy and shouting at the top of his voice.

"Look after the engine!" screamed Rose.

They were flying along now, for the river was narrowing and its current increasing with every yard. The wind could not reach the surface here, between the cliffs. Most of the surface was smooth and sleek like greased metal, but here and there were ominous furrows and ripples betraying the hidden inequalities of its bed. Rose steered carefully through the smooth water. She found she had to make ample allowance for leeway now; so fast was the current that the boat went flying down broadside on towards these obstructions in the course of the turn. There was another bend close ahead, a very sharp one from all appearance. She dragged the tiller across, she found she was not satisfied with her field of view ahead, and leaped up onto the bench, holding the tiller down by her right knee. With her left hand she reached up and tore the rotten canvas awning from it stanchions. They neither of them noticed the last two shots which the German captain of reserve fired at them at this moment.

The *African Queen* slithered round the corner, and lurched and rolled and heaved as she encountered the swirls which awaited her there. But the steady thrust of her screw carried her through them; that was Allnutt's job, to see that the launch had steerageway to take her through the eddies and to enable Rose to steer some sort of course with the following current.

There were rocks in the channel now, with white water boiling round them, and Rose saw them coming up towards her with terrifying rapidity. There was need for instant decision in picking the right course, and yet Rose could not help noticing, even in that wild moment, that the water had lost its brown colour and was now a clear glassy green. She pulled the tiller over and the rocks flashed by. Lower down, the channel was almost obstructed by rocks. She saw a passage wide enough for the boat and swung the bows into it. Stretching down before her there was a long green slope of racing water. And even as the *African Queen* heaved up her stern to plunge down it she saw that at the lower end of the fairway a wicked black rock just protruded above the surface — it would rip the whole bottom out of the boat if they touched it. She had to keep the boat steady on her course for a fraction of a second, until the channel widened a trifle, and then fling herself on the tiller to swing her over. The boat swayed and rocked, and wriggled like a live thing as she brought the tiller back again to straighten her out. For a dreadful second it seemed as if the eddy would defeat her efforts, but the engine stuck to its work and the kick of the propeller forced the boat through the water. They shaved through the gap with inches to spare, and the bows lurched as Rose fought with the tiller and they swung into the racing eddies at the tail of the rapid. Next moment they had reached the comparative quiet of the deep, fast reach below, and Rose had time to sweep the streaming sweat from her face with the back of her left forearm.

All the air was full of spray and of the roar of rushing water, whose din was magnified by the cliffs close at either side. The sound was terrifying to Allnutt, and so were the lurches and lunges of the boat, but he had no time to look about him. He was far too busy keeping the engine running. He knew, even better than did Rose, that their lives depended on the propeller giving them steerageway. He had to keep the steam pressure well up and yet well below danger point; he had to work the feed pump; he had to keep the engine lubricated. He knew that they would be lost if he had to stop the engine, even for a second. So he bent to his work with panic in his soul, while the boat beneath his feet leaped and bucked and lurched worse than any restive horse, and while, out of the tail of his eye, he could glimpse rocks flashing past with a speed which told him how great was their own velocity.

"Our Father Which art in Heaven —" said Allnutt to himself, slamming shut the furnace door. He had not prayed since he had left his Board School.

It was only a few seconds before they reached the next rapid, like the last a stretch of ugly rocks and boiling eddies and green, inclined slopes of hurtling water, where the eye had to be quick and the brain quicker still, where the hand had to be steady and strong and subtle and the will resolute. Halfway down the rapid there was a wild confusion of tossing water, in which the eye was necessarily slower in catching sight of those rocks just awash whose touch meant death. Rose rode the mad whirlwind like a Valkyrie. She was conscious of an elation and an excitement such as only the best of her brother's sermons had ever aroused. Her mind was working like a machine, with delirious rapidity. She forced the *African Queen* to obey her will and weave a safe course through the clustering dangers. The spray flew in sheets where the currents conflicted.

Lower down still, the river tore with incredible speed and without obstruction along a narrow gorge walled in with vertical faces of rock. To Rose, with a moment to think during this comparative inaction, it seemed as if this must be almost as fine as traveling in a motor car — an experience she had never enjoyed but had often longed for.

It was only for a moment that she could relax, however, for close ahead the gorge turned a corner, so sharply that it looked as if the river plunged into the rock face, and Rose had to make ready for the turn and brace herself to face whatever imminent dangers lay beyond, out of sight. She kept her eye on the rock at the water's edge on the inside of the bend, and steered to pass it close. So the *African Queen* was beginning to turn just before she reached the bend, and it was as well that it was so.

The sweep of the current took her over to the opposite bank as if she were no more than a chip of wood, while Rose tugged at the tiller with all her strength. The bows came round, but it looked for a space as if her stern would be flung against the rocks. The propeller battled against the current; the boat just held her own, and then as they drifted down, the backwash caught her and flung her out again into midstream, so that Rose had to force the tiller across like lightning, and hardly were they straight again than she had instantly to pick out a fresh course through the rocks that studded the surface in flurries of white foam.

Later she saw that Allnutt was trying to attract her attention. In the roar of the rapids he could not make his voice reach her. He stood up with one anxious eye still on his gauges, and he held up a billet of wood, tapped it, and waved a hand to the shore. It was a warning that fuel was running short, and fuel they must have. She nodded, although the next moment she had to look away and peer ahead at the rocks. They shot another series of rapids, and down another gorge where, the half-mile river compressed into fifty yards, they seemed to be traveling at the speed of a train. It was becoming vitally urgent that they should find somewhere to stop, but nowhere in that lightning six miles was there a chance of mooring. Allnutt was standing up brandishing his billet of wood again. Rose waved him impatiently aside. She was as much aware of the urgency of the situation as he was; there was no need for these continued demonstrations. They ran on, with Rose doggedly at the tiller.

Then she saw what she wanted. Ahead, a ridge of rocks ran almost across the stream, only broken in the centre, where the water piled up and burst through the gap in a vast green hump. Below the wings of this natural dam there was clear water — an absence of obvious rocks, at least; each corner was a circling, foam-striped eddy. She put the *African Queen* at the gap. The launch reared as she hit the piled-up water, put down her nose and heaved up her stern, and shot down the slope. At the foot were high green waves, each one quite stationary, and each one hard and unyielding. The launch hit them with a crash. Green water came boiling over the short deck forward and into the boat. Anyone with less faith than Rose would have thought that the *African Queen* was doomed to put her nose deeper and deeper, while the torrent thrust against the upheaved stern until she was overwhelmed. But at the last possible moment she lurched and wallowed and shook herself loose like some fat pig climbing out of a muddy pond. And even as she came clear Rose was throwing her weight on the tiller, her mind a lightning-calculating machine juggling with currents and eddies. The launch came round, hung steady as the tiller went back, shot forward in one eddy, nosed her way into another.

"Stop!" shrieked Rose. Her voice cut out like a knife through the din of the fall, and Allnutt, dazed, obeyed.

It was nicely calculated. The launch's residual way carried her through the edge of the eddy into the tiny strip of quite slack water under the lip of the dam. She came up against this natural pier with hardly a bump, and instantly a shaking Allnutt was fastening painters to rocks, half a dozen of them, to make quite sure, while the *African Queen* lay placid in the one bit of still water. Close under her stern the furious Ulanga boiled over the ridge; downstream it broke in clamour round a new series of rocks. Above the dam it chafed at its banks, and roared against the rocks which Rose had just avoided. All about them was frantic noise; the air was filled with spray, but they were at peace.

"Coo!" said Allnutt, looking about. Even he did not hear the word as he said it.

And Rose found herself weak at the knees, and with an odd, empty feeling in her stomach, and with such an aching, overwhelming need to relieve herself that she did not care if Allnutt saw her doing so or not.

One reaction followed another rapidly in their minds, but despite their weariness and hunger they were both of them conscious of a wild exhilaration. No one could spend half a day shooting rapids without exhilaration. There was a sense of achievement which affected even Allnutt. He was garrulous with excitement. He chattered volubly to Rose, although she could not hear a word he said, and he smiled and nodded and gesticulated, filled with a most unusual sense of well-being. This deep gorge was cool and pleasant. Up above, trees grew to the very edge of the cliffs, so that the light which came down to them was largely filtered through their leaves, and was green and restful. For once they were out of the sweltering heat and glare of Africa. There were no insects. There was no fear of discovery by the Germans.

With a shock Allnutt suddenly realized that only that morning they had been under fire; it seemed like weeks ago. He had to look round at the dangling funnel stay to confirm his memory, and automatically he went over to it and set himself to splice the broken wire. With that, the work of the boat got under way once more. Rose set up that wicked old hand pump and began to free the boat of the water which had come in; it slopped over the floor boards as they moved. But pumping in that restful coolness was not nearly as irksome as pumping on the glaring upper river. Even the pump, which one might have thought to be beyond reformation, was better behaved.

Allnutt climbed out of the boat in search of fuel, and any doubts as to the possibility of finding wood in the gorge were soon dispelled. There was driftwood in plenty. On shelves in the steep cliff, past floods had left wood in heaps, much of it the dry, friable kind which best suited the *African Queen*'s delicate digestion. Allnutt brought loads of it down to the boat, and to eke out this supply the slack water above the shore end of the dam was thick with sticks and logs brought down from above and caught up here. Allnutt fished out a great mass of it and left it to drain on the steep rocky side; by next morning it would be ready for use in the furnace, if helped out with plenty of the dry stuff.

Rose, in fact, had been really fortunate in finding the *African Queen* ready to her hand. The steam launch with all its defects possessed a self-contained mobility denied to any other method of transport. No gang of carriers in the forest could compare with her. Had she been fitted with an internal combustion engine she could not have carried sufficient liquid fuel for two days' running. As it was, taking her water supply from overside and sure of finding sufficient combustibles on shore, she was free of the two overwhelming difficulties which at that very moment were hampering the *Emden* in the Indian Ocean and were holding the *Königsberg* useless and quiescent in the Rufiji delta. Regarded as the captain of a raiding cruiser, Rose was happily situated. She had overcome her difficulties with her crew, and the stock of provisions heaped up in the bows showed as yet hardly a sign of diminution. She had only navigational difficulties to contend with; difficulties represented by the rocks and rapids of the lower Ulanga.

For the present neither Rose nor Allnutt cared about navigational difficulties in the future. They were content with what they had done that day. Nor did they moralize about the *African Queen*'s peculiar advantages. The everlasting roar of water in their ears was unfavourable to continuous thought, and rendered conversation quite impossible. They could only grin at each other to indicate their satisfaction, and eat enormously, and swill tea in vast mugs with lots of condensed milk and sugar — Rose found herself craving for sugar after the excitement of the day, and, significantly enough, made no effort to combat the craving. She had forgotten at the moment that any desire of the body should be suspect and treated as an instigation of the devil.

Freedom and responsibility and an open-air life and a foretaste of success were working wonders on her. She had spent ten years in Africa, but those ten years, immured in a dark bungalow, with hardly anyone save Samuel to talk to, had no more forwarded her development than ten years in a nunnery would have done. She had lived in subjection all her life, and subjection offers small scope to personality. And no woman with Rose's upbringing could live for ten days in a small boat with a man — even a man like Allnutt — without broadening her ideas and smoothing away the jagged corners and becoming something more like a human being. These last ten days had brought her into flower.

Those big breasts of hers, which had begun to sag when she had begun to lapse into spinsterhood, were firm and upstanding now again, and she could look down on them swelling out the bosom of her white drill frock without misgiving. Even in these ten days her body had done much towards replacing fat where fat should be and eliminating it from those areas where it should not. Her face had filled out, and though there were puckers round her eyes caused by the sun, they went well with her healthy tan, and lent piquancy to the ripe femininity of her body. She drank her tea with her mouth full, in a way which would have horrified her a month back.

When their stomachs were full, the excitement and fatigue of the day began to take effect. Their eyelids began to droop and their heads began to nod even as they sat with their dishes on their knees. The delicious coolness of the gorge played its part. Down between those lofty cliffs darkness came imperceptibly; they were once more in a land where there was twilight. Rose actually found herself nodding off fast asleep while Allnutt was putting the dishes away. The tremendous din of the water all round her was hardly noticed by her weary ears. For three nights now she had slept very badly in consequence of worrying about Allnutt. She felt now that she had nothing more to worry about; although the fire of her mission still burned true and strong she was supremely content. She smiled as she composed herself to sleep, and she smiled as she slept, to the blaring song of the Ulanga.

And Allnutt snuggled down on the boxes of explosive in a similar condition of beautiful haziness. What with fatigue and natural disability and the roar of the river he was in no condition for continuous thought, and the night before had been sleepless because of Rose's treatment of him. It was astonishing that it should be only the night before. It seemed more like a childish memory. After that had been settled they had come down past Shona. Coo, they had sucked the old Germans in proper. The poor beggars hadn't thought of shooting at them until they were past the town. Bet they were surprised to see the old *African Queen* come kiting past. They hadn't believed anyone would try to get down those gorges. Didn't believe nobody could. Well, this'd show 'em. Allnutt smiled too, in company with Rose, as he slid off into sleep to the music of the Ulanga.

It is a pretty problem of psychology to decide why Allnutt should have found a little manhood — not much, but a little — in Rose's society, among the broad reaches of the Ulanga, and in the roaring gorges, and under the fire of the German Askaris, when it had been so long denied him in the slums of his youth, and the stokeholds and engine rooms and brothels, and the easy-going condescension of the white men's mess of the Ulanga gold fields. The explanation may lie in the fact that Allnutt in this voyage so far had just sufficient experience of danger to give him a taste for it, so that he liked it while he hated it, paradoxically. Surfeit was yet to come.

Chapter 7

IT almost seemed, next morning, as if surfeit had come already. To look back on dangers past is a very different thing from looking forward to dangers close at hand and still to come. Allnutt looked at the roaring water of the fall, and at the rocky cataract which they would have to negotiate next, and he was frightened. There was an empty, sick feeling in his stomach and a curious feeling of pins and needles down the backs of his legs and in the soles of his feet. The next fifty yards, even, might find the boat caught on those rocks and battered to pieces, while he and Rose were beaten down by the racing current, crushed and drowned. He almost felt the strangling water at his nostrils as he thought about it. He had no appetite at all for breakfast.

But there was a vague comfort in the knowledge that there was nothing for them to do save go on. If they stayed where they were they would starve when their provisions came to an end. The only possible route to anywhere lay down the gorge. And the din of the water made it hard to think clearly. Allnutt got up steam in the boiler, and heaped the boat with fuel, and untied the painters with a feeling of unreality, as if all this was not really happening to him, although it was unpleasant.

Rose got up onto her seat and took the tiller. She studied the eddies of the pool in which they lay; she looked down the cataract which awaited them. There was no fear in her at all. The flutter of her bosom was caused by elation and excitement — the mere act of taking hold of the tiller started her heart beating faster. She gave directions to Allnutt by means of signs; a wave of her hand overside and Allnutt pushed off cautiously with the boat hook; she beckoned him to her and he put the engine into reverse for a revolution or two, just enough to get the bows clear. She watched the swirls and the slow motion of the launch backward towards the fall. Then she waved with a forward motion, and Allnutt started the propeller turning. The *African Queen* gathered slow headway, while the shaft vibrated underfoot. Rose brought the tiller over; the launch circled in the eddy, lurched into the main stream, and next moment was flying down with the current, and the madness of the day had begun.

That ability to think like lightning descended upon Rose's mind as they reached the main stream. She threaded her way through the rocks of the cataract as if it were child's play. It had become child's play to watch the banked-up white water round the rocks, to calculate the

speed of the current and the boat's speed through the
water, when to start the turn and what allowance to make
for the rebound of the water from the rock they were
passing in planning their approach to the next. The big
stationary wave which marked an underwater rock was
noted subconsciously. Mechanically she decided how
close to it she could go and what the effect of the eddy
would be.

Later, when the descent of the river was completed,
Rose found she could not remember the details of that
second day among the rapids with half the clearness of
the first. Those first rapids were impressed upon her
memory with perfect faithfulness; she could remember
every bend, every rock, every eddy; she could visualize
them just by closing her eyes. But the memories of the
second day were far more jumbled and vague. Rose only
remembered clearly that first cataract. The subsequent
ones remained in her mind only as long sequences of
roaring white water. There was spray which wetted her
face, and there were some nasty corners — how many she
could not tell. Her mind had grown accustomed to it all.

Yet the elation remained. There was sheer joy in crashing through those waves. Rose, with never a thought that
the frail fabric of the *African Queen* might be severely
tried by those jolts and jars, found it exhilarating to head
the launch into the stiff rigid waves which marked the
junction of two currents, and to feel her buck and lurch
under her, and to see the spray come flying back from the
bows. The finest sensation of all now was the heave

upwards of the stern as the *African Queen* reached the summit of one of those long, steep descents of green water and went racing down it with death on either hand and destruction seemingly awaiting them below.

Towards afternoon there was a cessation of cataracts. The river widened a trifle, but the walls of the gorge, although not quite so high, remained nearly vertical still. Between these walls the river raced with terrific velocity, but without impediment. There was time now to think and to enjoy oneself, to revel in the thrill of sending the *African Queen* skating round the corners, pushed far out by the current until the outside bank was perilously close to one's elbow. Even Allnutt, noticing the sudden smoothness of the passage, suspended his rigid concentration over the engine and raised his head. He watched in amazement the precipices flashing by at either hand, and he marveled at the dizzy way they slithered round the bends. There was something agonizingly pleasant about it. The feeling of constriction about the breast which he felt as he watched gave him an odd sense of satisfaction. He was full of the pride of achievement.

The mooring place which they desired presented itself along this cataract-free portion of the river. A tributary to the Ulanga came in here — not in any conventional way, but by two bold leaps down the precipice, to plunge bodily into the water after a forty-foot drop. Rose just had time to notice it, to steer clear and be drenched by the spray, when she saw that a sudden little widening of the channel just below, where the current had eaten away the rocky bank at a spot where the rock was presumably softer, offered them the assistance of a back eddy in mooring. She called to attract Allnutt's attention, signaled for half speed and then for reverse. Allnutt's boat hook helped in the manœuvre, and the *African Queen* came gently to a stop under the steep bank. Allnutt made fast the boat while Rose looked about her.

"How lovely!" said Rose, involuntarily.

She had not noticed the loveliness before; all that had caught her attention had been the back eddy. They had moored in what must have been one of the loveliest corners of Africa. The high banks here were not quite precipices, and there were numerous shelves in the rock bearing blue and purple flowering plants, which trailed shimmering wreaths down the steep faces. From the crest down to flood level the rock face was covered with the mystic blue of them. Higher upstream was the spot where the little tributary came foaming down the cliff face. A beam of sunlight reached down over the edge of the gorge and turned its spray into a dancing rainbow. The noise of its fall was not deafening; to ears grown used to the roar of the Ulanga cataracts it was just a pleasant musical accompaniment to the joyful singing of the calm, rapid river here. Under the rocky bank it was cool and delicious with the clear green river coursing alongside. The rocks were reds and browns and greys where they could be seen through the flowers, and had a smooth, well-washed appearance. There was no dust; there were no flies. It was no hotter than a summer noon in England.

Rose had never before found pleasure in scenery, just

as scenery. Samuel never had. If as a girl some bluebell wood in England (perhaps Rose had never seen a bluebell wood; it is possible) had brought a thrill into her bosom and a catch into her throat she would have viewed such symptoms with suspicion, as betokening a frivolity of mind verging upon wantonness. Samuel was narrow and practical about these things.

But Rose was free now from Samuel and his joyless, bilious outlook; it was a freedom all the more insidious because she was not conscious of it. She stood in the stern and drank in the sweet beauty of all, smiling at the play of colour in the rainbow at the waterfall. Her mind played with memories, of the broad, sun-soaked reaches of the upper Ulanga, of the cataracts and dangers they had just passed.

There was further happiness in that. There was a thrill of achievement. Rose knew that in bringing the *African Queen* down those rapids she had really accomplished something, something which in her present mood she ranked far above any successful baking of bread, or even (it is to be feared) any winning of infidel souls to righteousness. For once in her joyless life she could feel pleased with herself, and it was a sensation intoxicating in its novelty. Her body seethed with life.

Allnutt came climbing back into the boat from the shore. He was limping a little.

"D'you mind 'avin' a look at my foot, Miss?" he said. "Got a splinter in it up on the bank an' I dunno if it's all out."

"Of course," said Rose.

He sat upon the bench in the stern, and made to take off his canvas shoe, but Rose was beforehand with him. On her knees she slipped the shoe off and took his slender, rather appealing foot into her hands. She found the place of entry of the splinter, and pressed it with her finger tip while Allnutt twitched with ridiculous ticklishness. She watched the blood come back again.

"No, there's nothing there now," she said, and let his foot go. It was the first time she had touched him since they had left the mission.

"Thank you, Miss," said Allnutt.

He lingered on the bench gazing up at the flowers, while Rose lingered on her knees at his feet.

"Coo, ain't it pretty," said Allnutt. There was a little awe in his tone, and his voice was hardly raised loud enough to be heard above the sound of the river.

The long twenty-four hours spent in the echoing turmoil of the cataracts seemed to have muddled their thoughts. Neither of them was thinking clearly. Both of them felt oddly happy and companionable, and yet at the same time they were conscious something was missing, although they felt it close at hand. Rose watched Allnutt's face as he looked wondering round him. There was something appealing, almost childlike, about the little man with his dazed smile. She wanted to pet him, and then, noticing this desire in herself, she put it aside as not expressing exactly what it was she wanted, although she could find no better words for it. Both of them were breathing harder than usual, as though undergoing some strain.

"That waterfall there," said Allnutt, hesitatingly, "reminds me —"

He never said of what it reminded him. He looked down at Rose beside him, her sweet bosom close to him. He, too, was glowing with life and inspired by the awesome beauty of the place. He did not know what he was doing when he put out his hand to her throat, sunburned and cool. Rose caught at his hands, to hold them, not to put them away, and he came down to his knees and their bodies came together.

Rose was conscious of kisses, of her racing pulse and her swimming head. She was conscious of hands which pulled at her clothing and which she could not deny even if she would. She was conscious of pain which made her put up her arms round Allnutt's slight body and press him to her, holding him to her breasts while he did his will — her will — upon her.

Chapter 8

PROBABLY it had all been inevitable. They had been urged into it by all their circumstances — their solitude, their close proximity, the dangers they had encountered, their healthy life. Even their quarrels had helped. Rose's ingrained prudery had been drastically eradicated during these days of living in close contact with a man, and it was that prudery which had constituted the main barrier between them. There is no room for false modesty or physical shame in a small boat.

Rose was made for love; she had been ashamed of it, frightened of it, once upon a time, and had averted her eyes from the truth, but she could not maintain that suppression amid the wild beauty of the Ulanga. And once one started making allowances for Allnutt he became a likable little figure. He was no more responsible for his deficiencies than a child would be. His very frailties had their appeal for Rose. It must have been that little gesture of his in coming to her with a splinter in his foot which broke down the last barrier of Rose's reserve. And she wanted to give, and to give again, and to go on giving; it was her nature.

There was not even the difficulty of differences of social rank interposed between them. Clergyman's sister nowithstanding, there was no denying that Rose was a small tradesman's daughter. Allnutt's cockney accent was different from her own provincial twang, but it did not grate upon her nerves. She had been accustomed for much of her life to meet upon terms of social equality people with just as much accent. If Allnutt and Rose had met in England and decided to marry, Rose's circle might not have thought she was doing well for herself, but they would not have looked upon her as descending more than a single step of the social ladder at most.

Most important factor of all, perhaps, was the influence of the doctrine of the imperfection of man (as opposed to woman) which Rose had imbibed all through her girlhood. Her mother, her aunts, all the married women she knew, had a supreme contempt for men regarded in the light of house-inhabiting creatures. They were careless, and clumsy, and untidy. They were incapable of dusting a room or cooking a joint. They were subject to fits of tantrums. Women had to devote themselves to clearing their path for them and smoothing their way. Yet at the same time it was a point of faith that these incomprehensible creatures were the lords of creation for whom nothing could be too good. For them the larger portion of the supper haddock must always be reserved. For them on Sunday afternoons one must step quietly lest their nap be disturbed. Their trivial illnesses must be coddled, their peevish complaints heard with patience, their bad temper condoned. In fact — perhaps it is the explanation of this state of affairs — men were, in their inscrutable oddity, and in the unquestioned deference accorded them, just like miniatures of the exacting and all-powerful God Whom the women worshipped.

So Rose did not look for perfection in the man she loved. She took it for granted that she would not respect him. He would not be so dear to her if she did. If, as to her certain knowledge he did, he got drunk, and was not enamoured of a prospect of personal danger, that was only on a par with her father's dyspeptic malignity, or Uncle Albert's habit of betting, or Samuel's fits of cold ill-temper. It was not a question of knowing all and forgiving all, but of knowing all except that she was entitled to forgive. And these very frailties of his made an insidious appeal to the maternal part of her, and so did his corporal frailty, and the hard luck he had always experienced. She yearned for him in a way which differed from and reinforced the clamourings of her emancipated body. As the flame of passion died down in him, and, with his lips to her rich throat, he murmured a few odd, sleepy words to her, she was very happy, and cradled him in her strong arms.

Allnutt was very happy too. Whatever he might do in the heat of passion, his need was just as much for a mother as for a mistress. To him there was a comfort in Rose's arms he had never known before. He felt he could trust her and depend upon her as he had never trusted or depended upon a woman in his life. All the misery and tension of his life dropped away from him as he pillowed his head on her firm bosom.

Sanity did not come to them until morning, and not until late morning at that, and when it came it was only a partial sort of sanity. There was a moment in the early morning light when Rose found herself blushing at the memory of last night's immodesties, and filled with disquiet at the thought of her unmarried condition, but Allnutt's lips were close to hers, and her arms were about his slender body, and there was red blood in her veins, and memories and disquietude alike vanished as she caught him to her. There was a blushing interval when she had to own that she did not know his name, and, when he told her, shyly, she savoured the name "Charlie" over to herself like a schoolgirl, and she thought it a very nice name, too.

When the yearning for the morning cup of tea became quite uncontrollable — and after a night of love Rose found herself aching for tea just as much as after a day's cataract-running — it was she who insisted on rising and preparing breakfast. That "better portion of the haddock" convention worked strongly on her. She had not minded in the least having meals prepared by Allnutt her assistant, but it seemed wrong to her that Charlie (whom already she called "husband" to herself, being quite ignorant of the word "lover") should be bothered with domestic details. She felt supremely pleased and flattered when he insisted on helping her; she positively fluttered. And she laughed outright when he cracked a couple of jokes.

All the same, and in a fashion completely devoid of casuistry, Rose was appreciative of the difference between business and pleasure. When breakfast was finished she took control of the expedition again without a second thought. She took it for granted that they were going on, and that in the end they were going to torpedo the *König-in Luisa,* and it did not occur to Allnutt that now he occupied a privileged position he might take advantage of it to protest. He was a man simply made to be henpecked. What with the success they had met under Rose's command up to now, and with the events of the night, Rose's ascendancy over him was complete. He was quite happy to cast all the responsibility onto her shoulders and to await philosophically whatever destiny might send. He gathered fuel and he got up steam with the indifference engendered by routine.

Only when they were on the point of departure did either of them waver. Rose found him close beside her murmuring in a broken voice —

"Give us another kiss, old girl."

And Rose put her arms around him and kissed him, and whispered — "Charlie, Charlie, dear Charlie." She patted his shoulder, and she looked round at the beauty all about them, where she had given him her virginity, and her eyes were wet. Then they cast off, and Allnutt pushed off with the boat hook, and a second later they were in the mad riot of the Ulanga once more, coursing down between the precipices.

In some moment of sensible conversation that morning Allnutt had advanced the suggestion that the last cataract had been left behind and this portion of the river was merely the approach to the flat land round the lake. He proved to be wrong. After ten wild minutes of smooth water the familiar din of an approaching cataract reached Rose's ears. There was need to brace herself once more, to hold the tiller steady, and to stare forward to pick out the continuous line of clear water, a winding one to avoid the rocks and yet with no turn in it too sharp, which it was necessary to select in the few fleeting seconds between the sighting of the cataract and the moment when the *African Queen* began to heave among the first waves of the race.

So they went on down the wild river, deafened and drenched. Amazingly they survived each successive peril, although it was too much to hope that their luck would hold. They came to a place where the channel was too narrow and obstructed to offer in its whole width a single inch of clear water. Rose could only pick the point where the wild smother of foam was lowest, and to judge from the portions of the rocks exposed what course was taken by the water that boiled between them. The *African Queen* reared up and crashed into the tangle of meeting waves. She shook with the impact; water flew back high over the top of the funnel. Rose saw clear water ahead, and then as the launch surged through there was a crash beneath her, followed by a horrid vibration which seemed as if it would rattle the boat into pieces. With the instinct of the engineer Allnutt shut off steam.

"Keep her *going*, Charlie!" screamed Rose.

Allnutt opened the throttle a trifle. The devastating vibration began again, but apparently the propeller still revolved. The *African Queen* retained a little steerageway, while Allnutt prayed that the bottom would not be wrenched out of the boat. Rose, looking over the side, saw that they were progressing slowly through the water, while the current hurried them on at its usual breakneck speed. She could tell that it was vitally urgent that they should stop as soon as might be, but they were faced with the eternal problem of finding a mooring place in the narrow gorge with its tearing current. Certainly they must find one before the next cataract. With that small speed through the water she would never be able to steer the *African Queen* down a cataract; moreover, swinging the tiller experimentally, she found that something was seriously wrong with the steering. The propeller had a tendency now to swing the boat round crabwise, and it called for a good deal of rudder to counteract it. The cliffs streamed by on either side, while the clattering vibration beneath her seemed to grow worse, and she fought to keep the boat in mid-current. A long way ahead she could see the familiar dark rocks rearing out of the river, ringed at the base with foam. They *must* moor. Down on the left a big rock jutting out into the river offered them a tiny bit of shelter in the angle below it.

"Charlie!" she screamed above the roar of the river.

He heard her and understood her gesticulations. The

operation had to be timed to perfection. If they turned too soon they would be dashed onto the rock; if they turned too late they would miss the opportunity and would be swept, stern first and helpless, down the cataract. Rose had to make allowance for the changed speed of the boat, for this new twisting effect of the screw, for the acceleration of the current as it neared the cataract. With her lips compressed she put the tiller across and watched the bows anxiously as the boat came round.

It was too much to hope that the manœuvre would be completely successful. The bow came up behind the rock true enough, but the turn was not complete. The launch still lay partly across the river as her bow grounded in the angle. Instantly she heeled and rolled. A mass of water came boiling in over the gunwale. The boiler fire was extinguished in a wild flurry of steam, whose crackling was heard above the confusion of other sounds.

Allnutt it was who saved the situation. Grabbing the painter he leaped like an athlete, in a split second of time, nearly waist deep in a swirling eddy, and he got his shoulder under the bows and heaved like a Hercules. The bows slid off and the boat righted herself, wallowing three-quarters full of water; the tug of the current instantly began to take her downstream. Allnutt leaped up the face of the rock, still clutching the painter. He braced himself against the strain. His shoulder joints cracked as the rope tightened. His feet slipped, but he recovered himself. With another Herculean effort he made time for himself to get a purchase with the rope round an angle of the rock, and braced himself again. Slowly the boat swung in to shore, and the strain eased as the eddy began to balance the current. Five seconds later she was safe, just fitting into the little eddy behind the rock, as full of water as she could be without sinking, while Allnutt made painter after painter fast to the shore, and Rose still stood on the bench in the stern, the water slopping at her feet. She managed to smile at him; she was feeling a little sick and faint now that it was over. The memory of that green wave coming in over the gunwale still troubled her. Allnutt sat down on a rock and grinned back at her.

"We nearly done it that time," he said; she could not catch the words because of the noise of the river, but clearly he was not discomposed.

Allnutt was acquiring a taste for riverine dangers — rapid running can become as insidious a habit as morphine-taking — apart from his new happiness in Rose's society. Rose sat on the gunwale and kept her feet out of the water. She would not let her weakness be seen; she forced herself to be matter-of-fact. Allnutt swung himself on board.

"Coo, what a mess!" he said. "Wonder 'ow much we've lost."

"Let's get this water out and see," said Rose.

Allnutt splashed down into the waist and fished about for the bailer. He found it under the bench and handed it to Rose. He took the big basin out of the locker for himself. Before Rose got down to start bailing she tucked her skirt up into her underclothes as though she were a little girl at the seaside — the sensation of intimacy with Charlie, combating piquantly with her modesty, was extraordinarily pleasant.

The basin and the bailer between them soon lowered the level of the water in the boat; it was not long before Rose was getting out the wicked old hand pump to pump out what remained under the floor boards.

" 'Ere I'll do that, Rosie" said Allnutt.

"No, you set down and rest yourself," said Rose. "And mind you don't catch cold."

Pumping out the boat was about the nearest approach to dusting a room which could be found in their domestic life. Naturally it was not a man's work.

"First question is," said Allnutt, as the pumping drew to a close, " 'ow much does she leak?"

They pumped until the pump brought up no more water, while Allnutt addressed himself to getting up a couple of floor boards in the waist. A wait of half an hour revealed no measurable increase in the bilge.

"Coo blimy," said Allnutt. "That's better than we could 'ave 'oped for. We 'aven't lorst nothing as far as I can see, an' we 'aven't damaged 'er skin worth mentioning. I should 'ave fort there'd 'a' been a 'ole in 'er somewheres after what she's been through."

"What was all that clattering just before we stopped?" asked Rose.

"We still got to find that out, old girl," said Allnutt.

There was a cautious sympathy in his voice. He feared the very worst, and he knew what it would mean in disappointment to Rose. He had already looked up the

side of the ravine, and found a small comfort in the fact
that it was just accessible. If the *African Queen* was so
much disabled as he feared, they would have to climb up
there and wander in the forest until the Germans found
them — or until they starved to death. It said much for
his newfound manliness that he kept out of his voice the
doubts that he felt.

"How are we going to do that, dear?" asked Rose.

Allnutt looked at the steep bank against which they
were lying, and at the gentle eddy alongside.

"I'll 'ave to go underneath an' look," said he. "There
ain't no other wye, not 'ere."

The bank was steep-to. There was four feet of water
on the shore side of the boat, six feet on the river side, as
Allnutt measured it with the boat hook.

" 'Ere goes," said Allnutt, pulling off his singlet and
his trousers. They were wet through already, but it runs
counter to a man's instincts to immerse himself in water
with his clothes on.

"You stay 'andy wiv that rope, case there's a funny
current darn at the bottom."

Rose, looking anxiously over the side, saw his naked
body disappear under the bottom of the boat. His feet
stayed in view and kicked reassuringly. Then they grew
more agitated as Allnutt thrust himself out from under
again. He stood on the rocky bottom beside the boat, the
water streaming from his hair.

"Did you see anything, dear?" asked Rose, hovering
anxiously over him.

"Yerss," answered Allnutt. He said no more until he

had climbed back into the boat; he wanted time to compose himself. Rose sat beside him and waited. She put out her dry hand and clasped his wet one.

"Shaft's bent to blazes. Like a corkscrew," said Allnutt, dully. "An' there's a blade gone off the prop."

Rose could only guess at the magnitude of the disaster from the tone he used, and she underestimated it.

"We'll have to mend it, then," she said.

"Mend it?" said Allnutt. He laughed bitterly. Already in imagination he and Rose were wandering through the forest, sick and starving. Rose was silent before the savage despondency of his tone.

"Must 'a' just 'it a rock with the tip of the prop," went on Allnutt, more to himself than her. "There ain't nothink to notice on the deadwood. Christ only knows 'ow the shaft 'eld on while we was getting in 'ere. Like a bloody corkscrew."

"Never mind, dear," said Rose. The use of the words "Christ" and "bloody" seemed so oddly natural here, up against primitive facts, that she hardly noticed them, any more than she noticed Charlie's nakedness. "Let's get something dry, and have some dinner, and then we can talk about it."

She could not have given better advice. The simple acts of hanging things to dry, and getting out greasy tins from the boxes of stores, went far to soothe Allnutt's jangled nerves. Later, with a meal inside him, and strong tea making a hideous mixture in his stomach with bully beef, he felt better still. Rose returned them to the vital issue.

"What shall we have to do before we go on?" she asked.

"I'll tell you what we could do," said Allnutt, "if we 'ad a workshop, an' a landin' slip, an' if the parcel post was to call 'ere. We could pull this old tub out on the slip and take the shaft down. Then we might be able to forge it straight agine. I dunno if we could, though, 'cause I ain't no blacksmith. Then we could write to the makers an' get a new prop. They might 'ave one in stock, 'cause this boat ain't over twenty years old. While we was waitin' we might clean 'er bottom an' paint 'er. Then we could put in the shaft an' the new prop, an' launch 'er, an' go on as if nothink 'ad 'appened. But we 'aven't got nothink at all, an' so we can't."

Thoughts of the forest were still thronging in Allnutt's mind.

It was Rose's complete ignorance of all things mechanical which kept them from lapsing into despair. Despite Allnutt's depression, she was filled with a sublime confidence in his ability; after all, she had never yet found him wanting in his trade. In her mind the problem of getting a disabled steamboat to go again was quite parallel with, say, the difficulties she would meet if she were suddenly called upon to run a strange household whose womenfolk were down with sickness. She would have to get to know where things were, and deal with strange tradesmen, and accustom herself to new likes and dislikes on the part of the men. But she would tackle the job in complete confidence, just as she would any other household problem that might present itself. She might have to employ makeshifts which she hated; so might Allnutt. In her own limited sphere she did not know the word "impossible." She could not conceive of a man finding anything impossible in his, as long as he was not bothered, and given plenty to eat.

"Can't you get the shaft off without pulling the boat on shore?" she asked.

"M'm. I dunno. I might," said Allnutt. "Means goin' under water an' gettin' the prop off. *Could* do it, p'raps."

"Well, if you had the shaft up on shore you could straighten it."

"You got a hope," said Allnutt. "Ain't got no hearth, ain't got no anvil, ain't got no coal, ain't got nothink, an' I ain't no blacksmith, like I said."

Rose raked back in her memory for what she had seen of blacksmiths' work in Africa.

"I saw a Masai native working once. He used charcoal. On a big hollow stone. He had a boy to fan the charcoal."

"Yerss, I seen that, too, but I'd use bellers myself," said Allnutt. "Make 'em, easy enough."

"Well, if you think that would be better —" said Rose.

" 'Ow d'you mike charcoal?" asked Allnutt. For the life of him, he could not help entering into this discussion, although it still seemed to him to be purely academic — "all moonshine" as he phrased it to himself.

"Charcoal?" said Rose vaguely. "You set fire to great beehives of stuff — wood, of course, how silly I am — and after it's burnt there's charcoal inside. I've seen them do it somewhere."

"We might try it," said Allnutt. "There's 'eaps an' 'eaps of driftwood up on the bank."

"Well, then —" said Rose, plunging more eagerly into the discussion.

It was not easy to convince Allnutt. All his shop training had given him a profound prejudice against inexact work, experimental work, hit-or-miss work. He had been spoiled by an education with exact tools and adequate appliances; in the days of his apprenticeship, mechanical engineering had progressed far from the time when Stephenson thought it a matter of self-congratulation that the Rocket's pistons fitted her cylinders with only half an inch to spare.

Yet all the same, flattered by Rose's sublime confidence in him, and moved by the urgency of the situation, he gradually came round until he was half-disposed to try his hand on the shaft. Then suddenly he shied away from the idea again. Like a fool, he had been forgetting the difficulty which made the whole scheme pointless.

"No," he said. "It ain't no go, Rosie, old girl. I was forgetting that prop. It ain't no go wiv a blade gone."

"It got us along a bit just now," said Rose.

"Yerss," said Allnutt, "but —"

He sighed with the difficulty of talking mechanics to an unmechanical person.

"There's a torque," he said. "It ain't balanced —"

Any mechanic would have understood his drift at once. If a three-bladed propeller loses a blade, there are two blades left on one-third of its circumference, and nothing on the other two-thirds. All the resistance to its rotation under water is consequently concentrated upon one small section of the shaft, and a smooth revolution would be rendered impossible. It would be bad enough for the engine, and what the effect would be on a shaft fresh from the hands of an amateur blacksmith could be better imagined than described. If it did not break it would soon be again like the corkscrew of Allnutt's vivid simile. He did his best to explain this to Rose.

"Well, you'll have to make another blade," said Rose. "There's lots of iron and stuff you can use."

"An' tie it on, I serppose?" said Allnutt. He could not help smiling when his irony missed its mark altogether.

"Yes," said Rose. "If you think that will do. But couldn't you stick it on, somehow? *Weld* it. That's the right word isn't it? Weld it on."

"Coo, lumme," said Allnutt. "You are a one, Rosie. Reely you are."

Allnutt's imagination trifled with the idea of forging a propeller blade out of scrap iron, and hand-welding it into position, and affixing this botched propeller to a botched shaft, and then expecting the old *African Queen* to go. He laughed at the idea, laughed and laughed, so that Rose had to laugh with him. Allnutt found it so amusing that for the moment he forgot the seriousness of their position. Directly afterwards they found themselves in each other's arms — how, neither of them could re-member — and they kissed as two people might be ex-pected to kiss on the second day of their honeymoon.

They loved each other dearly, and cares dropped away from them for a space. Yet all the same, while Rose held Allnutt in her arms, she reverted to the old subject.

"Why did you laugh like that when I spoke about welding?" she asked in all seriousness. "Wasn't it the right word after all? You know what I mean, dear, even if it's not, don't you?"

"Crikey," said Allnutt. "Well, look here —"

There was no denying Rose; and Allnutt especially was not of the type to deny her. Moreover, Allnutt's mercurial spirits could hardly help rising under the influence of Rose's persistent optimism. The disaster they had experienced would have cast him into unfathomable despair if she had not been with him — despair, perhaps, which might have resulted in his not raising a finger to help himself. As it was, the discussion ended eventually, as was quite inevitable, in Allnutt's saying that "he would see what he could do," just as some other uxorious husband in civilization might see what could be done about buying a new drawing-room suite. And from that first yielding grew the hard week's work into which they plunged.

The first ray of hope came at the very beginning, when Allnutt, after much toil under water, with bursting lungs, managed to get the propeller off and out of the water. The missing blade had not broken off quite short. It had left a very considerable stump, two inches or so. In consequence it appeared more possible to bolt or fasten on a new blade — the propeller, of course, was of bronze, and as the new blade would have to be of iron there could be no question of welding or brazing. Allnutt put the propeller aside and devoted himself next to getting the shaft free; if he could not repair that it was useless to work on the propeller.

It was extraordinary what a prolonged business it was to free the shaft. Partly this was because it called for two pairs of hands, one pair inside the boat and one pair underneath the boat, and Rose had to be instructed in the use of spanners, and a very comprehensive code of signals had to be arranged so that Allnutt, crouching in the water underneath the boat, could communicate his wishes to her.

The need for all these signals was only discovered by trial and error, and there were maddening moments before they were fully workable.

The shaft was kinked in two places, close above and close below the bracket which held it steady, two feet from where it emerged from the glands, just above the propeller. There was no sliding it out through these bearings in either direction, as Allnutt discovered after a couple of trials. In consequence Allnutt had to work with spanner and screwdriver under water, taking the whole bracket to pieces, and, seeing that he had never set eyes on it in his life, and had to find out all about it by touch, it was not surprising that it took a long time. He would stand in the water beside the boat, his screwdriver in his hand and his spanner in his belt, taking deep breaths, and then he would plunge under, feel hastily for the bracket, and work on it for a few fleeting seconds before his breath gave out and he had to come out again.

The *African Queen* was moored in moderately still

water in the eddy below the rock, but only a yard or two away there was a racing seven-knot current tearing downstream, and occasionally some whim of the water expressed itself in a fierce underwater swirl, which swung the launch about and usually turned Allnutt upside down, holding on like grim death in case the eddy should take him out into the main current from which there would be no escape alive. It was in one of these swirls that Allnutt dropped a screw, which was naturally irreplaceable and must be recovered — it took a good deal of groping among the rocks beneath the boat before he found it again.

Before he had finished Allnutt developed a surprising capacity for holding his breath, and as a result of his prolonged immersions and exposures, his skin peeled off in flakes all over him. It was an important moment for Rose when at last, bending over the shaft in the bottom of the boat, she saw it slide out through the glands, and Allnutt emerged wet and dripping beside the boat with it in his hands.

Allnutt shook his head over the kinks and bends now revealed in the light of day — the terminal one was nearly half a right angle — but the two of them set themselves doggedly to the business of forging the thing straight again.

The sight of those kinks brought relief to Allnutt's mind in one respect. The fact that the metal had bent instead of breaking revealed that its temper was such that it might not suffer much from his amateur blacksmith's work — Allnutt was very well aware that what he knew about tempering was extraordinarily little. He comforted himself philosophically by telling himself that after all he was not dealing with a tool steel, and that obviously the shaft had a good deal of reserve strength, and that if he did not use extravagantly high temperatures and if he annealed the thing cautiously, he might not do too much harm.

There was not the slightest chance of their using very high temperatures, as they quickly discovered. Their attempts at making charcoal were complete and utter failures. When trying to reconstruct from memory what they had seen done, they soon discovered that they had seen with eyes unseeing. All they had to show in return for several piles of wood were heaps of white ashes and a few bits of what only a kindly person could have called charcoal. In desperation Allnutt resolved to try if he could not obtain a great enough heat with a wood fire and bellows. He made the bellows neatly enough with a couple of slabs of wood and an inch or two of piping and a pair of black, elbow-length gloves which Rose had carried in her tin box for ten years of Central Africa without wearing. When they found at last a good shape for their hearth of piled rocks Allnutt was relieved to discover that by energetic working of the bellows they could heat up that unwieldy shaft until he could actually alter its shape with his light hand hammer. They scorched themselves pretty well all over while using the flaring, inconsistent fuel, but all the same, the metal became soft enough to work in a

manner of speaking, and Allnutt was becoming reconciled to makeshifts by now.

Nevertheless, under the urging of the bellows, at
which Rose worked feverishly on her knees with
scorched face, the open hearth consumed wood at an incredible rate. It was not long before they had gathered in
every scrap of driftwood accessible in the ravine, and the
work was as yet hardly begun. They had to climb the
steep face of the ravine into the forest, and gather wood
there. The heat was sweltering, they were bitten by insects of all sorts, they wore themselves out and their
clothes into rags hacking paths through the undergrowth.
No one on earth could have climbed down that cliff face
with a load of wood; they had to drag the bundles to the
verge and push them over the edge, and some fell direct
into the river, and one or two caught on inaccessible
ledges and were lost just as thoroughly although they
were in sight, but they managed to profit by about half
the wood they collected in the forest.

Curiously enough, they were as happy as children
during these days of hectic work. Hard regular labour
suited both of them, and as soon as Allnutt had become
infected by Rose's passion to complete the job, they had a
common interest all day long. And every day there was
the blessed satisfaction of knocking off work in the late
afternoon, and revelling in the feeling of comradely
friendliness which drew them close together until passion
was aroused and hand went out to hand and lip met lip.
Rose had never known such happiness before, nor
perhaps had Allnutt either. They could laugh and joke

together; Rose had never laughed nor joked like that in the whole thirty-three years of her existence. Her father had taken shopkeeping as seriously as he (and her brother) had taken religion. She had never realized before that friendliness and merriment could exist along with a serious purpose in life, any more than she had realized that there was pleasure in the intercourse of the sexes. There was something intensely satisfying in their companionship.

Little by little that propeller shaft was straightened. Patient heating and patient hammering did their work. The major bends disappeared, and Allnutt turned his attention to the minor ones. He had to use a taut string now to judge of the straightness of the shaft, and he had to make himself a gauge of wire for testing the diameter, so nearly true was it, and there came a blessed morning when even his exacting mind was satisfied, and he pronounced the shaft was as good as he could make it. He could lay it aside now, and turn his attention to the far more difficult matter of the propeller blade.

In the end Allnutt made that new blade out of half a spare boiler tube. The operations on the shaft had taught him a good deal of the practical side of smith's work, and his experience with the propeller blade practically completed his education. Under the urging of necessity, and with the stimulus given him by Rose's confiding faith in his ability, Allnutt devised all sorts of ways of dealing with that boiler tube; it might almost be said that he reinvented some of his processes. He welded one end into a solid plate, and he worked upon it and beat it and shaped it until it gradually began to assume an appearance reminiscent of the other two blades which were his models.

The ravine rang with the sound of his hammer. Rose was his diligent assistant. She tended the fire, and worked the bellows, and, her hands shielded with rags, held the nominally cool end of the tube under Allnutt's instructions. Her nostrils were filled with the smell of scorching cloth, and she burned her fingers over and over again and nearly every single garment she and Allnutt possessed between them was burned and torn until they gave up the hopeless pursuit after decency, and she somehow enjoyed every minute of it.

There was intense interest in watching how the new blade took shape; there were exciting discussions as to how this difficulty or that was to be evaded. Allnutt found it all to his taste; there was gratification in the primitive pleasure of making things with his own hands.

"If my old dad," said Allnutt once, "had put me to blacksmithing when I was a kid, I don't think I should never have come to Africa. Coo! I might still —"

Allnutt lost himself in a pictured fantasy of a London working-class shopping district on a Saturday night, redolent with fried fish shops, garish with lights, and all a-bustle with people. He experienced a little qualm of homesickness before he came back to real life again, to the ravine with its pale red rocks, and the singing river, and the dazzling light, and the *African Queen* rocking in the eddy down below, and Rose beside him.

"But then I shouldn't never have met you, Rosie, old

girl," he went on. He fingered the embryo propeller blade. "Nor done all this. It's worth it. Every time it is, honest."

Allnutt would not have exchanged Rose for all the fried fish shops in the world.

Later the propeller blade began to demand accurate measurement, so like had it grown to its fellows. Allnutt had to invent gauges of intricate shape to make sure that the curvature and contour of the old blades were accurately reproduced, and before this part of the work was quite completed he turned his attention to the other end and set to work to forge a socket to fit over the broken stump, and to drilling holes by which it might be made comparatively safe. The moment actually came at last when the completed blade was slipped on over the stump, and Rose was given a practical demonstration of riveting — Allnutt made the rivets out of stumps of nail, and Rose had a trying time as "holder-on"; neither spanner nor pincers were really effective tongs.

The new blade was in position now, an exact match of its fellows, and to a casual inspection seemingly secure, but Allnutt was not yet satisfied. He could appreciate the leverage exerted upon a propeller blade in swift rotation, and the strain that would come under the base — upon his makeshift joint. At the risk of slightly reducing the propeller's efficiency he joined all three blades together with a series of triangles of wire strained taut. That would help to distribute the strain round the whole propeller.

"That ought to do now," said Allnutt. "Let's 'ope it does."

Putting the propeller shaft back into position, and settling it into its brackets, and putting on the propeller again, called for a fresh spell of subaqueous activity on the part of Allnutt.

"Coo, blimy," said Allnutt, emerging dripping at the side of the *African Queen*. "I oughter been a diver, not a blinkin' blacksmith. Let's 'ave that other spanner, Rosie, an' I'll 'ave another go."

Allnutt was very dear to her now, and she thought his remarks extraordinarily witty.

When shaft and propeller were in position, there was very little chance of testing the work. Once they left the bank they would have to go down the next cataract, willynilly. Allnutt got up steam in the boiler, and sent the propeller ahead for a few revolutions, until the mooring ropes strained taut, and then he went astern for a few revolutions more. It was good enough proof that shaft and propeller would turn, but it proved nothing else. It did not prove that the propeller would stand up to a full strain, nor that the shaft would not buckle under the impulse of a head of steam. They would have to find that out amid the rapids and cataracts, with certain death as their portion if Allnutt's work should fail them.

The night before, they had both of them visualized this situation, and they had neither of them ventured to discuss it. They had lain in each other's arms. Rose's eyes had been wet, and Allnutt's embrace had been urgent and possessive, each of them consumed with fear of losing the other. And this morning they tacitly acknowledged their danger, still without mentioning it. Steam was up, a full cargo of wood was on board, they were all ready for departure, Allnutt looked about him for the last time, at their rock-built hearth, and his rock-built anvil, and the heap of ashes that marked the site of one of their charcoal burning experiments. He turned to Rose, who was standing stiff and dry-eyed beside the tiller. She could not speak; she could only nod to him. Without a word he cast off the moorings, and held the *African Queen* steady in the eddy with the boat hook, while Rose scanned the surface of the river.

"Right!" said Rose, and her voice cracked as she said it. The sound of it hardly reached Allnutt's ears above the noise of the river and the hiss of steam. Allnutt pushed with the boathook, and as the bows came out into the current he gingerly opened the throttle.

"Goodbye, darling," said Allnutt, bent over the engine.

"Goodbye, darling," said Rose at the tiller.

Neither of them heard the other, and neither was meant to; there was a high courage in them both.

The *African Queen* surged out into the stream. For a moment they both felt as if something was wrong, because the shaft clanked no longer — it was straighter than it had been before the accident. Shaft and propeller held firm, all the same. The launch spun round as her bows met the current and Rose put the tiller across. Next moment they were flying downstream once more, with Allnutt attentive to the engine and Rose at the tiller, staring rigidly forward to pick her course through the weltering foam of the cataract ahead.

Chapter 9

❧

SOMEWHERE along their route that day they passed the spot where the Ulanga River changes its name and becomes the Bora. The spot is marked on no map, for the sufficient reason that no map of the country has ever been made, except for the hazy sketches which Spengler drew. Until Spengler and his Swahili boatmen managed to make the descent of the river by canoe no one had known, even if they had suspected it, that the big, rapid river which looped its way across the upland plateau and vanished into the gorges at Shona was the same as the stream which appeared in the tangled jungle of the Rift Valley a hundred miles from Shona and promptly lost itself again in the vast delta which it had built up for itself on the shore of the lake.

The native population, before the arrival of the Germans, had never troubled their heads about it. The delta of the Bora was a pestilential fever swamp; the rapids of the Ulanga were as Rose and Allnutt found them. No one in his senses would waste a minute's thought about one or the other, and since there was no practicable connection between the upper river and the lower it was of no importance whatever that they should happen to have different names.

When all was said and done, the difference in their names was justified by the difference in appearance. The change from the steep slope of the side of the Rift Valley to its flat bottom was most noticeable. The speed of the river diminished abruptly, and the character of the banks changed as well.

For the Ulanga, traveling at its usual breakneck speed, is charged with all sorts of detritus, and rolls much of its bed with it. No sooner does it reach the flat land than all its matter in suspension is dropped in the form of mud and gravel; the river spreads out, chokes itself with islands, finds new sluggish routes for itself. It is to be supposed that when the lake was first formed it lapped nearly up to the edge of the Rift Valley in which it lay, but for untold centuries the Ulanga — the Bora, as it must now be called — has deposited its masses of soil on the edge of its waters until a huge delta, as much as thirty miles along each of its three sides, has been formed, encroaching upon the lake, a dreary, marshy, amphibious country, half black mud and half water, steaming in a tropical heat, overgrown with dense vegetation, the home of very little animal life, and pestilent with insects.

Rose and Allnutt quite soon noted indications that

the transition was at hand. For some time the current was as fast as ever, and the stream as irregular, but the cliffs which walled it in diminished steadily in height and in steepness, until at last they were in no more than a shallow valley, with a vast creeper-entangled forest close at hand, and when they emerged from the shade, the sun blazed down upon them with a crushing violence they had not known in the sunless gorges of the upper river. The heat was colossal. Despite their motion through the stifling air they were instantly bathed in a sweat which refused to evaporate, and streamed down their bodies and formed puddles wherever its channel was impeded, and dripped into their eyes, and stung them and blinded them.

Rose was sweeping it from her face as she steered the *African Queen* down the last flurry of rapids — not the roaring cataracts she had once known, but a wider, shallower channel down which the water poured with a velocity deceptively great, and where tree trunks and shallows took the place of the foaming rocks of the upper river. There was still need for quick thinking and careful steering, because shallows grew up in the middle of the river, and the deep channels divided and redivided, coursing ever faster over the bottom, and growing ever shallower until at last the rocky ledge underneath was passed and the water slid over a steep sharp edge into water comparatively deep and comparatively slow.

Then there would be a respite for a time until a fresh change of colour in the water, and fresh danger signals ahead in the form of glittering patches of ripples, told of a new series of shallows approaching, and Rose had to plan a course for half a mile ahead, picking out some continuous deep channel, like a route through a maze, as far as the distant line of the steep edge. She knew enough about boats by now to guess that were she to choose a channel which died away into mere rushing shallows they would be hurried along until they bumped against the bottom, propeller and shaft damaged again, and probably, seeing how fast the river was running, the boat would be swung round, buried under the water piling against it, rolled over and torn to pieces while she and Charlie — she would not allow her mind to dwell on that, but bent her attention, with knitted brows, to seeing that the channels she chose did not come to that sort of end.

The weather changed with all the suddenness associated with the Rift Valley. Huge black clouds came rushing up the sky, intensifying the dampness of the heat until it could hardly be borne. Directly after came the lightning and the thunder, and the rain came pouring down, blotting out the landscape as effectively as a fog would do. At the first sight of the approaching storm Rose had begun to edge the *African Queen* in towards the shore, and the rain was just beginning when Allnutt got his boat hook into the stump of a huge tree which, still half alive, grew precariously on the edge of the water with half its roots exposed. The river had eaten away the bank all round it so that it formed a little island surrounded by dark, rushing water, and, swinging by their painter to this mooring, they sat uncomfortably through the storm.

The light was wan and menacing, the thunder rolled without ceasing to the accompaniment of a constant flicker of lightning. Yet the roar of the rain upon the boat and the river was as loud as the roar of the thunder. It beat upon them pitilessly, stupefying them. There was not even an awning now to offer them its flimsy shelter. All they could do was to sit and endure it, as if they were under the very heaviest type of lukewarm shower bath, hardly able to open their eyes.

The warm wind which came with the rain set the *African Queen* jerking at her painter despite the constant tug of the current, and before the storm had passed the wind blew from two thirds of the points of the compass, veering jerkily until at last Allnutt, blinded and stupefied though he was, had to get out the boat hook and hold the boat out from the shore lest the wind should blow her aground and imperil the shaft and propeller. Then at last the storm passed as quickly as it had come, the wind died away, and the afternoon sun came out to scorch them, setting the whole surface of the river steaming, and they could get out the pump and labour to empty the boat of the water which had filled it to the level of the floor boards.

With the cessation of the rain came the insects, clouds of them, hungry for blood, filling the air with their whining. Not even Rose's and Allnutt's experience of insects on the upper plateau had prepared them for an attack by these insects of the lower valley. They were ten times, twenty times, as bad as they had known them on the Ulanga; and moreover, their comparative freedom in the deep gorges had rendered them less accustomed and more susceptible still. Down here there was a type of fly new to them, a small black kind, which bit like a red-hot needle and left a drop of blood at every bite, and this type was as numerous as any of the dozen species of fly and mosquito which sang round them, flying into their eyes and their nostrils and their mouths, biting mercilessly at every exposed bit of skin. It was torment to be alive.

The coming of the evening and the sudden descent of night did nothing towards enfeebling their attacks. It seemed impossible to hope for sleep in that inferno of sticky heat under the constant torture of those winged fiends. The memory of yesterday's fairly cool, insect-free bed, when they had lain side by side in happy intimacy, seemed like the vague recollection of a dream. Tonight they shrank from contact with each other, writhing on their uncomfortable bed as if on the rack. Sleep seemed unattainable and yet they were both of them worn out with the excitement of the day.

Sometime in the night Allnutt rose and fumbled about in the darkness.

" 'Ere," he said. "Let's try this, old girl. It can't be no worse."

He had found the old canvas awning, and he spread it over the two of them, although it seemed as if they would die under any sort of covering. They drew the canvas about their faces and ears, streaming with sweat in the stifling heat. Yet the heat was more endurable than the insects. They slept in the end, half boiled, half suffocated; and they awoke in the morning with their heads swimming with pain, their joints aching, their throats constricted so that they could hardly swallow. And the insects still attacked them.

They had to wallow ashore through stinking mud to find wood, although it seemed agony to move; it took half a dozen journeys before the *African Queen* was fully charged with fuel again, sufficient to get them through the day. Already the sun was so hot that the floor boards seemed to burn their feet, and it was only Allnutt's calloused hands which could bear the touch of metal work. How he could bear the heat of the fire and the boiler was inconceivable to Rose; the heat which was wafted back to her in the stern was sufficient for her.

Yet being under way at least brought relief from insects. The speed of the *African Queen* was sufficient to leave that plague behind, and out in the middle of the river, half a mile broad here, there were no new ones to be found. It was worth enduring the sledgehammer heat of the sun for that.

The character of the river and the landscape was changing rapidly. Overside the water, which had regained its familiar brown tint of the upper reaches, was growing darker and darker until it was almost black. The current was noticeably less, and quite early in the day they ran the last of the rapids of the type they had encountered so frequently yesterday. That indicated the last rocky ridge extending across the bed of the river; they were definitely down the slope and in the bottom of the Rift Valley now.

There were no snags now; the river was far too deep. With its half-mile of width and sixty feet of depth the current slackened until it was almost unnoticeable, although a river engineer could have calculated that the volume of water passing a given point in a given time was equal to that higher up where the constricted shallow channel had raced between its precipices.

On either bank now appeared broad fringes of reeds — papyrus and ambatch — and beyond them belts of cane indicated the marshy banks, and beyond the cane could be seen the forest, dark and impenetrable. Out in the centre of the river there was silence save for the clatter of the engine and the breaking of the wash; the *African Queen* clove her way through the black water under the burning sun. In that vast extent of water they seemed to be going at a snail's pace; there were loops and bends in the river's course which they took a full two hours to get round — motiveless bends, to all appearance, for there was no alteration in the flat monotony of the banks.

Although there was no need now to keep watch against snags or rapids, there was still need for some degree of vigilance on Rose's part. Much of the surface of the river was cumbered with floating rubbish, tangles of weed and cane, branches and logs of wood which might imperil the propeller; the current was too slow here to force this flotsam out to the banks and strand it there. It was a relief from the monotony of steering to keep a lookout for the dangerous type of log floating almost entirely submerged; and soon Rose began to lay a course which took her close to each successive floating mass, and she and Allnutt were able to select and pull in those bits of wood of a size suitable for use in the fire. It comforted Rose's economical soul in some inexpressible way to render the *African Queen* by this means still more independent of the shore, and in point of fact, as Rose observed to herself, it was quite as well to maintain the supply of fuel as fully as possible, having regard to the marshiness and inaccessibility of the banks. The fuel they gathered in this way was sufficient to help considerably towards maintaining their stock in hand, even though it did not compensate for their whole consumption.

That day of monotonous sun and monotonous river wore slowly towards its close. Allnutt came aft with a surprising suggestion.

"We needn't tie up to the bank tonight, old girl," he said. "It's a muddy bottom, and we can use the anchor agine. I vote we anchor out 'ere. Mosquitoes won't find us 'ere. We don't want another night like last night if we can 'elp it."

"Anchor here?" said Rose. The possibility had not occurred to her. Five yards had been the farthest from land they had ever lain at night, and that was in the backwaters of the upper river — months ago, she felt. It seemed queer to stop in that tiny boat a quarter of a mile from land, and yet obviously there was no reason against it.

"All right" she said, at length.

"I won't stoke no more then, and where we stops we —"

"Anchors" was the word Allnutt was going to use,

but he did not have time to say it, some minor crisis in the engine summoning him forward on the jump. He turned and grinned reassurance to Rose after he had put matters right.

Gradually the beat of the engine grew slower and slower, and the *African Queen*'s progress through the water died away until it was almost imperceptible. All-nutt went forward and let go the anchor, which took out its chain with a mighty rattle that echoed across the river and brought flights of birds out from the forest.

"Not sure that it's touching bottom," said Allnutt philosophically. "But it doesn't matter. If we start driftin' near trouble, that ole anchor'll stop us before the trouble gets too near. There ain't nothing that can 'urt us in sixty foot o' water. Now for Christ's sake let's rig up somethink to give us a bit o' shade. I seen enough o' that sun to last me a lifetime."

The sun was still blazing malignantly down on them, although the day was so far advanced, but Allnutt stretched the remains of the awning overhead and a rug along the awning stanchions, and there was a blessed patch of shade in the sternsheets in which they could recline with their eyes shielded from the persistent glare. As Allnutt had predicted, they were nearly free from the mosquito curse here; the few insects that came to bite were almost unnoticeable to people who had endured the assault of millions yesterday.

Rose and Allnutt could even endure contact with each other again now; they could kiss and be friendly. Rose could draw Allnutt's head down to her breast, and clasp him to her in a new access of emotion. Later on when peace had descended upon them they could talk together, in quiet voices to suit the immense silence of the river.

"Well," said Allnutt. "We done it, old girl. We got down the Ulanga all right. I didn't think it could be done. It was you who said we could. If it 'adn't been for you, sweet'eart, we shouldn't be 'ere now. Don't yer feel prard o' yerself, dear?"

"No," said Rose, indignantly. "Of course not. It was you who did it. Look at the way you've made the engine go. Look how you mended the propeller. It wasn't me at all."

Rose really meant what she said. She was actually beginning to forget the time when Allnutt had been found wanting, to forget the time when she had had to coerce him by silence into continuing the voyage. In some ways this was excusable, for so much had happened since then; if Rose had not known that it was only three weeks since the voyage had started she would have guessed it to be at least three months. But her forgetfulness was due to another cause as well; she was forgetting because she wanted to forget. Now that she had a man of her own again it seemed unnatural to her that she should have forgotten her femininity so far as to have made plans, and coerced Allnutt, and so on. It was Charlie who ought to have the credit.

"I don't think," she said, very definitely indeed, "there's another man alive who could have done it."

"Don't think anyone's likely to try," said Allnutt, which was a very witty remark and made Rose smile.

"We'll have a good supper tonight," said Rose, jumping up. "No, don't you move, dear. You just sit still and smoke your old cigarette."

They had their good supper, all of the special delicacies which the Belgian manager of the mine received in his fortnightly consignment — tinned tomato soup, and tinned lobster, and a tin of asparagus, and a tin of apricots with condensed milk, and a tin of biscuits. They experimented with a tin of *pâté de foie gras,* but neither of them liked it, and by mutual consent they put it overside half finished. And, swilling tea afterwards, they were both of them firmly convinced that they had dined well. They were of the generation and class which had been educated to think that all good food came out of tins, and their years in Africa had not undeceived them.

The night came down and the river stretched on either side, immeasurable and vast in the starlight. The water was like black glass, unruffled by any wind, and deep within it the reflection of the stars glowed like real things. They fell into a dreamlike state of mind in which it was easy to believe that they were suspended high above the earth, with stars above and stars below; the gentle motion of the boat as they moved helped in the illusion.

"Coo!" said Allnutt, his head on Rose's shoulder. "Ain't it lovely?"

Rose agreed.

Yet for all this hypnotic peace, for all the love they bore each other, in the hearts of both was the determination of war. Rose's high resolve to clear the lake of England's enemies burned as high as ever, unexpressed though it might be. Von Hanneken would not continue long to flaunt the iron cross flag unchallenged on Lake Wittelsbach if she could prevent it. Every little while she thought of those gas cylinders and boxes of explosive up in the bow with a quiet confidence, in the same way as she might in other circumstances think of a store-cupboard shelf full of soap laid up ready for spring cleaning. There was no flaunting ambition about it, no desire to rival the fame of Florence Nightingale or Grace Darling or Joan of Arc. It was a duty to be done, comparable with washing dishes. Rose asked nothing more of life than something to do.

For details, Charlie would have to attend to those — fuses and explosives were more in a man's line. Charlie would see to it all right. It was a perfectly natural gesture that at the thought of Charlie making an efficient torpedo she should clasp his arm more tightly to her, evoking in response a grunt of peaceful satisfaction.

That uxorious individual had no will of his own left now. What little there was had evaporated by the second day of shooting the rapids, the day when Rose had miraculously admitted him to her arms. He was content to have someone to admire and to follow. Even though Rose had no thought of rivalling Joan of Arc she resembled her in this power she exerted over her staff. The last few days had been one long miracle in Allnutt's eyes. Her complete fearlessness in the wild rapids which had turned his bowels to water affected him indescribably.

There was constantly present in his mind's eye the remembered picture, a composite formed during hundreds of anxious glances over his shoulder, of Rose erect at the tiller, vigilant and unafraid amidst the frantic turmoil of the cataracts — it was the lack of fear, not the vigilance, which impressed him so profoundly. She had not been cast down when the propeller broke. Her confidence had been unimpaired. She had been quite sure he could mend it, although he had been quite sure he could not, and behold, she was right. Allnutt was by now quite sure that she would be right again in the matter of torpedoing the *Königin Luise,* and he was ready to follow her into any mad adventure to achieve it.

The very intimacy to which she admitted him, her tenderness for him, confirmed him in this state of mind. No other woman had been tender to Charlie Allnutt, not his drunken mother, nor the drabs of the East End, nor the enslaved prostitutes of Port Said, nor Carrie, his mistress at the mine, whom he had always suspected of betraying him with the filthy native labourers. Rose was sweet and tender and maternal, and in all this she was different from everyone else. He could abandon all thought of himself and his troubles while he was with her. It did not matter if he was a hopeless failure as long as she forbore to tell him so.

When she pressed his arm he held her more closely to reassure himself once more, and her kiss brought him peace and comfort.

Chapter 10

⊶

To the tranquillity of the night succeeded the fever of the day. No sooner had the sun climbed up out of the forest than it began to pour its heat with insane violence upon the little boat exposed upon the broad face of the river. It demanded attention in a manner that would take no denial. The discomfort of immobility in the sun was such that the instinctive reaction was to make instant preparations to move somewhere else, even though bitter experience taught that there was no relief in movement — even the reverse in fact, in consequence of the need for firing up the boiler.

They headed on down the wide black river. Everything was still; the surface was glassy as they approached it. Behind them the ripples of their course and their spreading wake left a wedge-shaped area of disturbed water, expanding farther and farther until a long way astern, almost as far as the eye could see, it reached the reedy banks. They went on through the breathless heat, winding eternally round the vast motiveless bends of the river. There was just enough mist prevailing to make the distance unreal and indistinct.

Rose brought the *African Queen* slowly round one more bend. The mist was thicker here. She could not determine the future course of the river, whether at the end of this reach it turned to the left or to the right. It did not matter here, where the river was so wide and so deep. Tranquilly she held on down the middle of the channel, a quarter of a mile from either shore. She could be sure of seeing the direction of the next bend when it came nearer.

Only slowly did it dawn upon her that the river had widened. In that misty heat the banks looked much the same at half a mile as at a quarter of a mile. Undoubtedly they were further from both banks now. It did not matter. She kept the *African Queen* to her old course, heading for the mist-enshrouded forest right ahead. She was sure that sooner or later they would open up the next reach.

Somehow even half an hour's steaming did not reveal the channel. They were nearing the dark green of the forest and the brighter green strip of the reeds now. Rose could see a vast length of it with some precision, but there was no break. She came to the conclusion that the river must have doubled nearly back upon itself, and she put the tiller over to starboard to approach the left hand bank again. There was no satisfaction to be found here. There was only the unbroken bank of reeds and the eternal forest, and moreover, something in the contour of that sky line seemed to tell her that it was not in this direction that the river found an exit.

For a moment she dallied with the idea that perhaps the river ended altogether somewhere in this neighbourhood, but she immediately put the notion aside as ridiculous. Rivers only end thus abruptly in deserts, not in rain-beaten forests of this sort. This was German Central Africa, not the Sahara. She looked back whence they had come, but the last stretch of comparatively narrow river was at least three miles back by now, low down on the horizon and shrouded with mist and out of sight.

There was only one course to adopt which promised definite results. She put the tiller over again and began to steer the *African Queen* steadily along the edge of the fringe of reeds. Whatever happened to the river she was bound to find out if she kept along its bank for long enough.

"D'you think this is the delta, dearie?" called Allnutt from the bows. He was standing on the gunwale looking over the wide expanse of water.

"I don't know," said Rose, and added, doggedly, "I'll tell you soon."

Her notion of a delta was a lot of channels and islands, not a lake five miles wide with no apparent outlet.

They steamed along the fringe of reeds. A change in the character of the water became noticeable to Rose's eye, practised through many long days in watching the surface. It was black water here, and although it had been black enough a little higher up, there was something different about it. It was lifeless, lacklustre water here. There were long curling streaks upon it indicative of some infinitely slow eddy circling in its depths. There was far more trash and rubbish afloat on the surface than usual. In fact there seemed every indication that here they had reached, in defiance of all laws of nature, an ultimate dead end to the river.

"Beats me to guess where we've come to," said Allnutt. "Anywye, there's a nell of a lot of wood 'ere. Let's stop and fill up while we can."

It was not at all difficult to collect a full charge of fuel of all the sorts Allnutt liked, from the long dead stuff which would give a quick blaze to solid boughs which could be relied upon to burn for a considerable time. Allnutt fished the wood out of the water. Even here, a mile from solid land, there was insect life to be found. He shook all sorts of semi-aquatic little creatures off it as he lifted it in. With his axe he cut it into handy lengths, as well as he could in the boat, and spread it out to dry over the floor boards. Only an hour or two in that blazing sun was necessary to bring even waterlogged wood into such a condition that it would burn.

"I should fink we got enough now, Rosie," said Allnutt at last.

They continued their journey along the reeds. Rose was conscious that she was steadily bringing the tiller over to port. They must be making a wide curve round the edge of this lake; a glance at the sun told her that they were heading in a direction nearly opposite to the one in which they had entered. On their left hand the bank of reeds grew wider and wider, so wide in fact that it was hard to see any details of the forest beyond it. Yet as a half-mile river must make an exit somewhere along here Rose remained confident, despite her wavering doubts, that sooner or later they would come to a break. Strangely, there was no break to be seen as the afternoon wore on. Here and there were vague indications of tiny channels through the reeds, but they were very indefinite indeed. Certainly they were not passages clear of reeds; it was only that the reeds were sparser, as though there were a deeper bit of water up to the shore in which only the tallest reeds could hope to reach the surface. The forest was too distant and dense for any indication to show there.

The only break in the monotony came when they scared a herd of hippopotamuses, twenty or so of the beasts, in a wild panic through water, reeds, and mud, until they all with one accord took cover beneath the surface and vanished as mysteriously as they had appeared. Rose had hardly a thought or a look for the hippopotamuses. She was thinking too hard about this extraordinary behaviour of the river. She was still using port helm to keep them at a constant distance from the bank. As far as she could judge by the sun they were now nearly on the same course as they had been when she had first noticed the widening of the river. They must in consequence have come round almost in a full circle.

To confirm this opinion she looked over to starboard, at the opposite bank which had been barely in sight a quarter of an hour ago. It was nearer now, far nearer. At the end of another ten minutes the horrid suspicion was confirmed. They were back again at the mouth of the river, at the point of its emergence into the lake. She only had to starboard the helm to head the *African Queen* upstream, towards the rapids whence they had come. It was a shock to her. A week or two ago she might have wept with humiliation and disappointment, but she was of sterner stuff now; and after her recent experiences there was hardly anything an African river could do which would surprise her.

As a matter of fact, her mistake was perfectly excusable, as the behaviour of the Bora and one or two other rivers which flow into Lake Wittelsbach is very unusual, and is the result of the prolific character of the aquatic vegetation of tropical African. The channels of the delta of the Bora are narrow, floored with rich silt, and with hardly any current to scour them — ideal conditions in that climate for the growth of water weed. As a result the channels are nearly choked with weeds and reeds, the flow through them grows less and less, and the river finds itself dammed back at its outlet.

As a result it banks up into a lagoon behind its delta. The slight increase in pressure which follows does, in the end, force some of the water out through creeks and channels winding a precarious way through the delta, but the lagoon itself increases in size with the steady inflow from the river until in the end it turns the flank of the delta on one side or the other, and bursts its way through into the lake by a new mouth. Then the level of the lagoon drops sharply, the current through this new channel diminishes in proportion, and the whole process is resumed, so that in the progress of centuries the delta extends itself steadily from side to side.

In 1914, when Rose and Allnutt came down the river, it was fifteen years since the last time the Bora had made a new mouth for itself, the lagoon was nearly at its maximum size, and the few channels which remained unchoked were so overgrown and winding that there was really nothing surprising at Rose's missing them. She was not the fool she felt herself to be in that bitter moment.

She was soothed to some extent by the stupidity of Allnutt. He, engrossed in the supervision of the engine, had paid only small attention to their course. When Rose called to him to stop he was surprised. Looking about him at the wide river he quite failed to recognise it. He thought Rose had found the outlet to the lake which they had entered at a different point. It was only when Rose made him drop the anchor and showed him that the slight, hardly perceptible current was running in the opposite direction to the one he wished to take that he admitted his mistake.

"These blinking banks look all one to me," he said.

"They do to me too," said Rose, bitterly, but Allnutt remained cheerfully optimistic.

"Anywye," he said. " 'Ere we are. We got a good mooring agine for tonight, old girl. No mosquitoes. We might just as well be comfy and forget abart things for a bit."

"All right," said Rose.

Yet she went on standing on the gunwale, one hand on the awning stanchion and the other shading her eyes, staring across the lagoon at the distant opposite shore, veiled in its greyish purple mist.

"That's where the way out must be" she decided. "A lot of little channels. I noticed quite a lot through the reeds, and wouldn't take them. Where we saw those hippos. We'll pick the best one tomorrow, and get through somehow. It can't be very far to the lake."

If English explorers had turned back at the sight of apparent impossibilities the British Empire would not be nearly its present size.

The night was not of the tranquillity which had characterized the preceding one. Rose was discontented with the day's progress, and filled with a vague disquiet about her capacity as a pilot. She was not used to failure, and was annoyed with herself. Even at the end of two hour's peace in the shade of the awning and screen which Allnutt rigged, she had not regained her optimism. Instead, she was merely filled with a bitter determination to fight her way through that delta cost what it might, or to die in the attempt — a resolution which hardened the set of her mouth and made her conversation with Allnutt a little abstracted, and made sleep slow in coming.

And just as distracting was the sound of the frogs in the reeds. Hereabouts there must have been a colony of thousands, millions, of the little brutes, to whom presumably the attraction of the place lay in the suitability of the still water for spawning. They croaked in unison; Rose could distinguish two distinct kinds of croak, a deep-voiced kind whose volume never altered, and a higher-pitched kind which waxed and waned with monotonous regularity. Despite the distance of the boat from the reeds, the din of the croaking came over the water to them as loud as the noise of a heavy surf on a reef, and with much the same variations of loudness and pitch. It was an infuriating noise, and it went on all night.

It did not disturb Allnutt, for no accountable noise could do that, and Allnutt's peaceful sleeping was nearly as annoying as the croaking of the frogs to Rose in her wakefulness. She lay and sweated in the breathless night, disturbed, uncomfortable, irritated. If Rose had ever indulged in scolding or shrewishness she would have been an evil companion the next morning, but a rigid upbringing had had sufficient effect on her to prevent her from indulging in such a wanton abuse of power. She did not yet know she could scold; she had never tasted the sweet delights of giving rein to ill temper.

Instead, she was only curt and impatient, and Allnutt, after a sidelong glance at her in response to some brief reply of hers to his loquaciousness, had the sense to hold his tongue. He wagged his head to himself and felt immensely wise, as he pondered over the inscrutable ways of womanhood, and he saw to it that steam was raised and the boat made ready for departure with the smallest possible delay.

Rose steered the *African Queen* straight out across the lagoon towards the place where she had decided she would find the best way through the delta. The low band of trees across the horizon grew more and more distinct.

Soon they could distinguish the rich lush green of the reeds.

"Go slower now!" called Rose to Allnutt, and the beat of the engine slackened as Allnutt closed the throttle.

She took a course as close along the margin of the reeds as she dared. She did not like the appearance of them at all, pretty though they were. They grew in tough-looking, solid clumps, each stalk expanding at the top into a rather charming flowerhead, and, apart from a few bold outliers, the clumps grew close together, while farther in towards the shore they were crowded in a manner which would make progress through them practically impossible. She did not know that probably this very species had provided the "bulrushes" which composed the ark in which Moses had been set afloat on the Nile, nor that the learning of the world was most deeply indebted to it for the paper it had provided all through antiquity; and if she had known she would not have cared. All she sought was a way through.

Twice she hesitated as they neared points where the reeds did not grow quite so thickly, but each time she held on past them; there was the channel beyond through the forest of the delta to be considered as well. Such trivial indications of a waterway meant that its continuation through the delta might be impassable. Then they reached a broader, better-defined passage. Rose raked back through her memory and decided this was at least as good as any she had noticed yesterday. She put the tiller over and turned the nose of the boat into the opening.

Nervously, Allnutt closed the throttle until the propeller was hardly revolving, and the *African Queen* glided among the reeds at a snail's pace; Rose nodded approval, for they did not want to run any risks with that patched propeller. The channel remained fairly clear of reeds as it wound this way and that. Sometimes a clump scraped along the side with a prodigious rustling; Allnutt was sounding overside with the boat hook. It seemed that providentially the reeds refused to grow in water a little deeper than the *African Queen*'s draught; a channel which was clear of them was just navigable for her.

There came the inevitable moment when the channel bifurcated and a choice had to be made. Rose stared out over the sea of reeds at the nearing trees and brought the boat round into the most promising channel. They glided on; at each side the growth of reeds became denser and denser. And then the *African Queen* seemed to hesitate in her progress; there was something different about the feel of her, and Allnutt reached hastily to the throttle and shut off steam.

"We're aground, dearie," he said.

"I know that," snapped Rose. "But we've got to go on."

Allnutt poked at the bottom with the boat hook; it was deep, semi-liquid mud. There was no hope in consequence of their getting out and towing her, which was the first idea which occurred to him. He displayed the dripping boat hook to Rose.

"We must pull her along by the reeds," she said, harshly. "The keel will go through mud like that even though we can't use the propeller."

They addressed themselves to the task, Rose reaching

out with her hands to the clumps she could reach, and Allnutt with the boat hook. Soon their technique improved with experiment and experience. The papyrus reed grows from a long, solid root which extends a considerable distance horizontally in the mud before turning upwards to form the head. Perched up in the bows, Allnutt reached forward with the boat hook, fumbled about until he found a good grip, and then tugged the boat forward for a couple of feet through the ooze. Then he had to abandon the root he had found and search for a new one to gain another couple of feet.

It was terribly hot work among the reeds, which were not high enough to give shade although they cut off what little wind there was, and the sun glared down upon them with its noonday intensity. And soon the insects found them; they came in clouds until the air was thick with them, mad with the thirst for blood. The work was heavy and tiring, too. Two hours of it left Allnutt gasping for breath, and whenever he gasped he spluttered, in consequence of the insects he had drawn into his mouth.

"Sorry, Miss," he said at last, apologetically. "Can't keep on at this, not any'ow."

The face he turned towards Rose was as wet with perspiration as if he had been under a shower bath; so were his rags of clothes. Neither he nor Rose noticed his use of "Miss" — it sounded perfectly natural from a beast of burden such as he had become.

"All right," said Rose. "Give me the boat hook."

"The work's a bit 'eavy," said Allnutt, with a note of protest in his tone.

Rose took no notice, but climbed past him on to the little foredeck, the boat hook in her hand. Allnutt made as if to argue further, but did not. He was too exhausted even to argue. He could only sink down into the bottom of the boat and lie there with the sweat drip-drip-dripping about him. For Rose he had, literally, worked until he dropped. Rose certainly found the work heavy. Reaching forward to get a grip with the boat hook was a strain. To get the boat to move forward over the mud and the reed roots called for the exertion of every particle of strength she possessed — convulsive effort, to be followed immediately by the need for another, and another after that, interminably.

It did not take very long to exhaust her completely. In the end she put down the boat book with a clatter and reeled down the boat into the waist, her clothes hanging about her in wet wisps. The flies followed her, in myriads.

"We'll go on again tomorrow," she gasped to Allnutt, who opened his eyes at her as he slowly came back to normality.

The reeds were higher about them now, for in their progress under this new method of traction they had practically left the papyrus behind and were come into the territory of another genus, and the sun was lower. They were in the shade at last; the boat, which had seemed as hot as a gridiron to the touch, became almost bearable, and the flies bit worse than ever. In time Rose recovered sufficiently to try to find out how close they were to the shore. She climbed on the gunwale, but the giant reeds stretched up over her head, and she could see nothing but reeds and sky. How far they had come, how far they were from the forest, she could not guess. She certainly had not anticipated taking a whole day to get through a belt of reeds a mile wide, but here was the first day ended and as far as she could tell they were only half-way in, and there was nothing to indicate that they would ever get through at all. No matter. They would go on try-ing tomorrow.

Anyone less stout-hearted than Rose might have be-gun to wonder what would happen to them if their for-ward progress became impossible. There was no chance at all of their pulling the boat back stern first the way they had come. They would be held there until they starved like trapped animals, or until they drowned themselves in the mud and slime beneath the reeds, trying to make their way ashore on foot. Rose did not allow that sort of notion to trouble her. Her resolution was such that no mere possibility could alarm her. She was like Napoleon's ideal general in that she did not make pictures of what might be — just as, all through this voyage, she had acted on Nelson's dictum "lose not an hour." If following, how-ever unconsciously, the advice of the greatest soldier and the greatest sailor the world has ever seen would bring success to this land and water campaign, success would be theirs. And if they failed it would not be through lack of trying — that was what Rose was vowing to herself as she fought the flies.

Chapter 11

THERE had been no need to moor the boat that night. No ordinary manifestation of Nature could have stirred her far from where she lay among those tall reeds. The wind that came with the thunderstorm that night was hardly felt by them at all — it bowed the reeds across the boat, but sitting beneath the arch they formed they did not notice the wind. They had to endure all the discomforts of the rain as it poured down upon them in the dark, but even in those miserable conditions the ruling passion of that quaint pair displayed itself again.

"One thing abart this rine," said Allnutt during a lull. "It my deepen the water in this 'ere channel — if you can call it a channel. This afternoon we wasn't drorin' much more than there was 'ere. 'Alf a inch would mike a 'ell of a big difference. It can't rine too much for me, it can't."

Then later that night, when the rain had long ceased, and Allnutt had somehow got to sleep despite the mosquitoes, Rose was suddenly aware of a noise. It was only the tiniest, smallest possible murmur, and only the ear of faith could have heard it through the whining of the mosquitoes. It was the noise of running water. From all around there came this gentle sound, slighter than the quietest breathing — water seeping dribbling through the reeds as the level rose in the lagoon, helped on by the gathered rain which the Bora was bringing down. Rose almost woke up Allnutt to listen to it, but refrained, and contented herself with vowing to make an early start in the morning so as to take full advantage of any rise before it could leak away through the delta — although seeing that they always started at the first possible moment it is hard to understand what Rose meant by an "early start."

There was this much variation, all the same, in their routine on rising that morning, in that they did not have to spend time in firing up the boiler and getting up steam. The sun was still below the tall reeds when they were ready to start, and already before Allnutt had come up into the bows to resume his yesterday's toil Rose was standing there, gazing into the reeds, trying to make out what she could about their course.

There really was no denying that they were still in some sort of waterway leading through the reeds. It was ill-defined; all there was to be seen was a winding line along which the reeds grew less densely, but it surely must lead somewhere.

"I fink she's afloat," said Allnutt with satisfaction, taking the boat hook.

He reached out, found a hold, and pulled. There seemed to be a freer movement than yesterday.

"No doubt about it," reported Allnutt. "We got all the water we want. If it wasn't for these blasted reeds —"

The channel was narrower here than when they had entered it, and the reeds caught against the sides as they moved along. Some had to be crushed under the boat, with the result that as each pull progressed the boat met with an increasing resistance; sometimes, maddeningly, she even went back an inch or two as Allnutt sought for a fresh grip. The resistance of the reeds, all the same, was far less unrelenting than the resistance of yesterday's mud, and Rose was able to be of some help by hastening about the boat freeing the sides from the reeds which impeded them.

They crawled on, slowly but hopefully. From what they could see of the sun there was no doubt that they were preserving a certain general direction towards the delta. Suddenly there came a squeal of joy from Allnutt.

"There's another channel 'ere!" he said, and Rose scrambled up into the bows to see.

It was perfectly true. The channel they were in joined at an acute angle a similar vague passage way through the reeds, and the combined channel was broader, better defined, freer from reeds. As they looked at its dark water they could see that the fragments afloat on it were in motion — as slow as a slow tortoise, but in motion nevertheless.

"Coo!" said Allnutt. "Look at that current! Better look out, Rosie, old girl. It'll be rapids next."

They could still laugh.

Allnutt drew the *African Queen* into the channel. It was delightful to feel the boat floating free again, even though she could not swing more than an inch to either side. He hooked a root and gave a hearty pull; the boat made a good four feet through the water, and, what was more, retained her way, creeping along steadily while All-nutt sought for a new purchase.

"Blimy," said Allnutt. "We're going at a rate of knots now."

A little later, as they came round a bend in the channel, Rose caught sight of the trees of the delta. They were instantly obscured again by the reeds, but the next bend brought them in sight again, not more than two hundred yards off, and right ahead. She watched them coming nearer. Almost without warning the passage through the reeds widened. Then, abruptly, the reeds ceased, and the *African Queen* drifted sluggishly forward for a yard or two and then stopped. They were in a wide pool, bordered on the farther side by dark trees, and the surface of the pool was covered with water lilies, pink and white, growing so closely that it seemed as if the whole pool was a mass of vegetation.

The sunlight was dazzling after the green shade of the reeds; it took a little while for their eyes to grow accustomed to the new conditions.

"That's the delta all right," said Allnutt, sniffing.

A dank smell of rotting vegetation came to them across the water; the farther bank was a wild tangle of trees of nightmare shape, wreathed with creepers.

"We won't 'alf 'ave a gime getting this old tub through that lot," said Allnutt.

"There's a channel over that way," said Rose, pointing. "Look!"

There certainly was some sort of opening into the forest there; they could see white water lilies blooming in the entrance.

"I s'pect you're right," said Allnutt. "All we got to do now, in a manner of speaking, is to get there."

He remembered the last water lily pool they had encountered, high up on the Ulanga. There, all they had to do was to get out again having once entered. Here there was a hundred yards of weed-grown water to traverse.

"Let's try it," said Rose.

"Course we're going to try it," answered Allnutt, a little hurt.

It was not easy — nothing about that voyage to the lake was easy. Those water lily plants seemed to yield at a touch of the boat hook, and afforded no purchase at all by which they could draw themselves along. Yet at the same time they clung so thick about the boat as to limit its progress as much as the reeds had done. Allnutt darkly suspected from the behaviour of the boat that they were being caught upon the screw — that precious screw with the weak blade — and rudder. The bottom was of such liquidity that it offered practically no resistance to the thrust of the boat hook when used as a punt pole, and in drawing the pole out again Allnutt found that he pulled the boat back almost as much as he had previously shoved it forward. Volleys of gas bubbles rose whenever the boat hook touched the bottom; the stink was atrocious.

"Can't we try rowing?" asked Rose. Time was passing with the rapidity they always noticed when progress was slow, and they had hardly left the edge of the pool.

"We might," said Allnutt.

One item in the gear of the *African Queen* was a canoe paddle. Allnutt went forward and found it, and gave it to Rose. He brought back a billet of firewood for his own use.

Paddling the boat along made their progress a little quicker. There could be nothing slapdash nor carefree about wielding a paddle in those weeds. It had to be dipped carefully and vertically, reaching well forward, and it had to be drawn back with equal care, without twisting, lest at the moment of withdrawal it should be found so entangled as to call for the use of a knife to free it.

It was not a rapid method of transport. Rose would note some cluster of blooms up by the bows, and it would be at least a minute's toilsome work before it was back alongside her. Nor was the *African Queen* adapted for paddling. She had to sit on the bench in the stern-sheets twisted uncomfortably sideways; a few minutes' paddling set up a piercing ache under her shoulder blade like the worst kind of indigestion. She and Allnutt had continually to change sides for relief.

So slowly did they move that when they came completely to a standstill they neither of them realized it at once, and went on paddling while the suspicion grew until they looked round at each other through the streaming sweat and found each had been thinking the same thing.

"We're caught up on something," said Allnutt.

"Yes."

"It's that ole prop. Can't wonder at it in this mess."

They stood together at the side of the boat, but of course there was no judging the state of affairs from there.

"Only one thing for it," said Allnutt. He took out his knife, opened it, and looked at its edge.

"A spot of diving is the next item on the program, li-dies and gents," he said. He tried to grin as he said it.

Rose wanted to expostulate; there was danger in that massed weed, but Allnutt must chance the danger if the voyage was to go on.

"We'll have to be careful," was all she could say.

"Yerss."

Allnutt fetched a length of rope.

"We'll tie that round my waist," he said, as he stripped off his clothes. "You count firty from the time I go under, an' if I ain't coming up by then, you pull at that rope, an' pull, an' pull, an' go on pulling."

"All right," said Rose.

Allnutt sat naked on the gunwale and swung his legs over.

"Good crocodile country this," he said, and then, seeing the look on Rose's face, he went on hastily. "Nao it ain't. There ain't no croc. on earth could get through these weeds."

Allnutt was not too sure about it himself. He was ris-ing to an unbelievable height of heroism in what he was doing. Not even Rose could guess at the sick fear within him, but in reaction from his cowardice he was growing foolhardy. He took his knife in his hand and dropped into the water. Holding on to the gunwale, he breathed deeply half a dozen times, and then ducked his head under the boat. His legs vanished under the carpet of weed, while Rose began to count with trembling lips. At "thirty" she began to pull on the rope, and she sighed with relief as Allnutt emerged, all tangled with weed. He had to put up a weed-clustered hand to pull a mask of the stuff from his face before he could breathe or see.

"There's a lump like a beehive round that prop," he said as he gasped for breath. "An' 'alf the weeds in the lake are anchored on to it."

"Is it any use trying to clear it?"

"Ooh yerss. Stuff cuts easy enough. I'd done a good bit already when I 'ad to come up. Well, 'ere goes agine."

At the fourth ascent Allnutt grinned with pleasure.

"All clear," he said. " 'Old the knife, will you, old girl? I'm comin' in."

He pulled himself up over the gunwale with Rose's assistance. The water streamed off him and from the masses of weed which clung to his body. Rose fussed over him, helping to pick him clean. Suddenly she gave a little cry, which was instantly echoed by Allnutt.

"Just look at the little beggars!" said Allnutt — the swearwords he still refrained from using were those which, never having come Rose's way, she did not know to be swearwords.

On Allnutt's body and arms and legs were leeches, a

score or more of them, clinging to his skin. They were swelling with his blood as Rose looked at them. They were disgusting things. Allnutt was moved at the sight of them to more panic than he had felt about crocodiles.

"Can't you pull 'em off?" he said, his voice cracking. "Arhh! The beasts!"

Rose remembered that if a leech is pulled off before he is gorged he is liable to leave his jaws in the wound, and blood poisoning may ensue.

"Salt gets them off" she said, and sprang to fetch the tin in which the salt was kept.

Damp salt dabbed on the leeches' bodies worked like magic. Each one contorted himself for a moment, elongated himself and thickened himself, and then fell messily to the floor boards. Allnutt stamped on the first one in his panic, and blood — his own blood — and other liquid spurted from under his foot. Rose scooped the remains and the other leeches up with the paddle and flung them into the water. Blood still ran freely from the triangular bites, drying in brown smears on Allnutt's body under the blazing sun; it was some time before they could induce it to clot at the wounds, and even when it was all over Allnutt was still shuddering with distaste. He hated leeches worse than anything else on earth.

"Let's get awye from 'ere," was all the reply he could make to Rose's anxious questionings.

They paddled on across the lily pool. With the coming of the afternoon some of the pink blooms began to close. Other buds opened, ivy-coloured buds with the

faintest tinge of blue at the petal tips. That carpet of lilies
was a lovely sight, but neither of them had any eyes for its
beauty. They sank into a condition of dull stupidity, their
minds deadened by the sun; they said nothing to each
other even when they exchanged places. Their course
across the pool was as slow as a slug's in a garden. They
dipped and pulled on their paddles like mechanical con-
trivances, save when their rhythm was broken by the
clutch of the maddening weeds upon the paddles.

The sun was lower by now; there was a band of shade
on the rim of the pool which they were approaching.
With infinite slowness the *African Queen*'s nose gained
the shade. Allnutt nerved himself for a few more strokes,
and then, as the shade slid up to the stern and reached
them, he let fall his billet of wood.

"I can't do no more," he said, and he laid his head
down upon the bench.

He was nearly weeping with exhaustion, and he
turned his face away from Rose so that she would not see.
Yet later on, when he had eaten and drunk, his cockney
resilience of spirits showed itself despite the misery the
mosquitoes were causing.

"What we want 'ere," he said, "is a good big cataract.
You know, like the first one below Shona. We'd 'ave got
'ere from the other side of the reeds in about a minute
an' a 'alf, I should say, 'stead of a couple of dyes an' not
there yet."

Later in the evening he was facetious again.

"We've come along under steam, an' we've paddled,

an' we've pushed, an' we've pulled the ole boat along wiv the 'ook. What we 'aven't done yet is get out an' carry 'er along. I s'pose that'll come next."

Rose remembered those words, later in the following day, and thought they had tempted Providence.

Chapter 12

———∞———

IN the morning there was only a narrow strip of water-lily lake to cross under the urgings of the early sun. They fought their way across it with renewed hope, for they could see the very definite spot where the lilies ceased to grow, and the beginning of a channel through the delta, and they felt that no obstacle to navigation could be as infuriating and exhausting as those lilies.

The delta of the Bora is a mangrove swamp, for the water of Lake Wittelsbach, although drinkable, is very slightly brackish, sufficiently so for some species of mangrove to grow, and where mangroves can grow there is no chance of survival for other trees. Where the mangroves began, too, the water lilies ended, abruptly, for they could not endure life in the deep shade which the mangroves cast.

They reached the mouth of the channel and peered down it. It was like a deep tunnel; only very rare shafts of light from the blazing sky above penetrated its gloomy depths. The stench as of decaying marigolds filled their nostrils. The walls and roof of the tunnel were composed of mangrove roots and branches, tangled into a fantastic conglomeration of shapes as wild as any nightmare could conceive.

Nevertheless, the repellent ugliness of the place meant no more to them than had the beauty of the water lilies. These days of travel had obsessed them with the desire to go on. They were so set upon bringing their voyage to its consummation that no place could be beautiful that presented navigational difficulties, and they were ready to find no place ugly if the water route through it were easy. When they crashed out from the last clinging embrace of the water lilies they both with one accord ceased paddling to look into the water, each to his separate side.

"Coo," said Allnutt, in tones of deep disgust. "It's grass now."

The weed which grew here from the bottom of the water was like some rank meadow grass. The water was nearly solid with it. The only encouraging feature it displayed was that the long strands which lay along the surface all pointed in the direction in which they were headed — a sure sign that there was some faint current down the channel, and where the current went was where they wanted to go too.

"No going under steam 'ere," said Allnutt. "Never get the prop to go round in that muck."

Rose looked down the bank of mangroves, along the

edge of the lily pool. They might try to seek some other way through the delta, but it seemed likely that any other channel would be as much choked with weed, while any attempt to find another channel would involve more slow paddling through water lilies. She formed her decision with little enough delay.

"Come on," was all she said. She had never heard Lord Fisher's advice "Never explain," but she acted upon it by instinct.

They leant forward to their work again and the *African Queen* entered into the mangrove swamp with the slowness to be expected of a steam launch moved by one canoe paddle and one bit of wood shaped rather like a paddle.

It was a region in which water put up a good fight against the land which was slowly invading it. Through the mangrove roots which closed round them they could see black pools of water reaching far inwards; the mud in which the trees grew was half water, as black and nearly as liquid. The very air was dripping with moisture. Everything was wet and yet among the trees it was as hot as in an oven. It made breathing oppressive.

"Shall I try 'ooking 'er along, now, Rosie?" said Allnutt. He was refusing to allow the horror of the place to oppress his spirits. "We get along a bit better that wye."

"We could both of us use hooks here," said Rose. "Can you make a hook?"

"Easy," said Allnutt. Rose was fortunate in having an assistant like him.

He produced a four-foot boat hook quickly enough, beating the metal hook out of an angle iron from an awning stanchion, binding it tightly to the shaft with wire.

With both of them using hooks their progress grew more rapid. They stood side by side in the bows, and almost always there was a root or branch of the mangroves within reach on one side or the other, or up above, so that they could creep along the channel, zigzagging from side to side. Reckoning the mangrove swamp as ten miles across, and allowing fifty per cent. extra for bends in the channel, and calling their speed half a mile an hour — it was something like that — thirty hours of this sort of effort ought to have seen them through. It took much longer than that, all the same.

First of all, there were the obstructions in the channel. They encountered one almost as soon as they entered among the mangroves, and after that they recurred every few hundred yards. The *African Queen* came to a standstill with a bump and a jar which they came to know only too well — some log was hidden in the black depths of the water, stretching unseen across the channel. They had to sound along its length. Sometimes, when they were fortunate, there was sufficient depth of water over it at some point or other to float the boat across, but if there was not they had to devise some other means of getting forward. The funnel early came down; Allnutt dismantled that and the awning stanchions quite soon in consequence of the need for creeping under overhanging branches.

Generally, if the channel were blocked they could find some passage round the obstruction through the pools of water which constituted a sort of side channel here and there, but to work the *African Queen* through them called for convulsive efforts, which usually involved Allnutt's disembarking and floundering in the mud, and warping the launch round the corners. It was as the *African Queen* was slithering and grating over the mud and the tree roots that Allnutt's ill-omened words about getting out and carrying the boat recurred to Rose's mind.

If there were no way over or round they had to shift the obstruction in the channel somehow, ascertaining its shape and weight and attachments by probings with the boat hooks, heaving it in the end, with efforts which in that Turkish bath atmosphere made them feel as if their hearts would burst, the necessary few inches this way or that. They grew ingenious at devising methods of rigging tackle to branches above, and fixing ropes to the obstructions beneath, so as to sway the things out of their way. And Allnutt, perforce, overcame his shuddering hatred of leeches — on one occasion they squatted in mud and water for a couple of hours, while with knives they made two cuts in a submerged root which barred the only possible bit of water through which they could float the *African Queen.*

It was a nightmare time of filth and sludge and stench. Be as careful as they would, the all-pervading mud spread by degrees over everything in and upon the boat, upon themselves, everywhere, and with it came its sickening stink. It was a place of twilight, where everything had to be looked at twice to make sure what it was, so that, as every step might disturb a snake whose bite would be death, their flounderings in the mud were of necessity cautious.

Worse than anything else, it was a place of malaria. The infection had probably gained their blood anew in the lower reaches of the Bora, before they reached the delta, but it was in the delta that they were first incapacitated. Every morning they were prostrated by it, almost simultaneously. Their heads ached, and they felt a dull coldness creeping over them, and their teeth began to chatter, until they were helpless in the paroxysm, their faces drawn and lined and their finger nails blue with cold. They lay side by side in the bottom of the boat, with the silent mangrove forest round them, clutching their filthy rags despite the sweltering steamy heat which they could not feel. Then at last the cold would pass and the fever would take its place, a nightmare fever of delirium and thirst and racking pain, until when it seemed they could bear no more the blessed sweat would appear, and the fever die away, so that they slept for an hour or two, to wake in the end capable once more of moving about — capable of continuing the task of getting the *African Queen* through the Bora delta.

Rose dosed herself and Allnutt regularly with quinine from the portable medicine chest in her tin trunk; had it not been for that they would probably have died, and their bones would have mouldered in the rotting hull of the *African Queen* among the mangroves.

They never saw the sun while they were in that twilight nightmare land, and the channel twisted and turned so that they lost all sense of direction, and had no idea at all to which point of the compass they were heading. When the channel they were following joined another one, they had to look to see which way the water was flowing to decide in which direction to turn, and where it was so dark that even the water grass would not grow, as happened here and there, they had to note the direction of drift of bits of wood placed on the surface — an almost imperceptible drift, not more than a few yards an hour.

It was worse on the two occasions when they lost the channel altogether as a result of forced detours, through pools round obstacles. That was easy enough to do, where every tangle of aërial roots looked like every other tangle, where the light was poor and there was nothing to help fix one's direction, and where to step from the islands of ankle-deep slime meant sinking waist deep in mud in which the hidden roots tore the skin. When they were lost like this they could only struggle on from pool to pool, if necessary cutting a path for the boat with the axe by infinite toil, until at last it was like paradise to rejoin a murky, root-encumbered channel on which they might progress as much as fifty yards at a time without being held up by some obstacle or other.

They lost all count of time in that swamp. Days came and went, each with its bout of chill and fever; it was day when there was light enough to see, and night when the twilight had encroached so much that they could do no more, and how many days they passed thus they never knew. They ate little, and what they ate stank of the marshes before they got it to their mouths. It was a worse life than any animal's, for no animal was ever set the task of coaxing the *African Queen* through those mangroves — with never a moment's carelessness, lest that precious propeller should be damaged.

No matter how slippery the foothold, nor how awkward the angle of the towrope, nor how imminent an attack of malaria, the launch had always to be eased round the corner inch by inch, without a jerk, in case during her lateral progress the propeller should be swung sideways against some hidden root. There was never the satisfaction of a vicious tug at the rope or a whole-hearted shove with the pole.

They did not notice the first hopeful signs of their progress. The channel they were in was like any other channel, and when it joined another channel it was only what had happened a hundred times before; they presumed that there would be a bifurcation further on. But when yet another large channel came in they began to fill with hope. The boughs were thinning overhead so that it grew steadily lighter; the channel was deep and wide, and although it was choked with water grass that was only a mere trifle to them now, after some of the obstacles they had been through, and they had developed extraordinary dexterity at hooking the *African Queen* along by the branches. They did not dare to speak to each other as the channel wound about, a full ten feet from side to side.

And then the channel broadened so that real sunlight reached them, and Allnutt could wait no longer before speaking about it, even if it should be unlucky.

"Rosie," he said. "D'you fink we got through, Rosie?"

Rose hesitated before she spoke. It seemed far too good to be true. She got a good hold on an aërial root and gave a brisk pull which helped the *African Queen* bravely on her way, before she dared to reply.

"Yes," she said at length. "I think we have."

They managed to smile at each other across the boat. They were horrible to look at, although they had grown used to each other. They were filthy with mud — Rose's long chestnut hair, and Allnutt's hair, and the beard which had grown again since they had entered into the delta, were all matted into lumps with it. Their sojourn in the semi-darkness had changed their deep sunburn into an unhealthy yellow colour which was accentuated by their malaria. Their cheeks were hollow and their eyes sunken, and through the holes in their filthy rags could be seen their yellow skins, with the bones almost protruding through them. The boat and all its contents were covered with mud, brought in by hurried boardings after negotiating difficult turns. They looked more like diseased savages of the Stone Age than such products of civilization as a missionary's sister and a skilled mechanic. They still smiled at each other, all the same.

Then the channel took another turn, and before them there lay a vista in which mangroves played hardly any part.

"Reeds!" whispered Allnutt as though he hardly dared to say it. "Reeds!"

He had experienced reeds before, and much preferred them to mangroves. Rose was on tiptoe on the bench by now, looking over the reeds as far as she could.

"The lake's just the other side," she said.

Instantly Rose's mind began to deal with ways and means, as if she had just heard that an unexpected guest was about to arrive to dinner.

"How much wood have we got?" she asked.

"Good deal," said Allnutt, running a calculating eye over the piles in the waist. " 'Bout enough for half a dye."

"We ought to have more than that," said Rose, decisively.

Out on the lake there would not be the ready means of replenishment which they had found up to now. The *African Queen* might soon be contending with difficulties of refuelling beside which those of Müller and Von Spee would seem child's play. There was only one effort to be asked of the *African Queen,* but she must be equipped as completely as they could manage it for that effort.

"Let's stop here and get some," she decided.

To Allnutt, most decidedly, and to herself in some degree, the decision was painful. Both of them, now that they had seen a blue sky and a wide horizon, were filled with a wild unreasoning panic. They were madly anxious to get clear away from those hated mangroves without a second's delay. The thought of an extra hour among them caused them distress; certainly, if Allnutt had been by himself he would have dashed off and left the question of fuel supply to solve itself. But as it was he bowed to Rose's authority, and when he demurred it was for the general good, not to suit his own predilections.

"Green wood's not much good under our boiler, you know," he said.

"It's better than nothing," replied Rose. "And I expect it'll have a day or two to dry off before we want it."

They exchanged a glance when she said that. All the voyage so far had been designed for one end, the torpedoing of the *Königin Luise*. That end, which had seemed so utterly fantastic to Allnutt once upon a time, was at hand now; he had not thought about it very definitely for weeks, but the time was close upon him when he would have to give it consideration. Yet even now he could not think about it in an independent fashion; he could only tell himself that quite soon he would form some resolve upon the matter. For the present he had not a thought in his head. He moored the *African Queen* up against the mangroves and took his axe, and cut at the soft pulpy wood until there was a great heap piled in the waist. And then at last they could leave the mangroves for the happy sanctuary of the reeds.

Chapter 13

─ ∞∞∞ ─

*I*T was a very definite mouth of the Bora by which they had emerged. There was a fair wide channel through the reeds, and they had no sooner entered it and turned one single corner than the limitless prospect of the lake opened before them — golden water as far as the eye could see ahead, broken by only one or two tree-grown islands. On either side of the channel were shoals, marked by continuous reeds, extending far out into the lake, but those they could ignore. There was clear water, forty miles broad and eighty long, in front of them, not a rock nor a shoal nor a water lily nor a reed nor a mangrove to impede them — unless they should go out of their way to seek for them. The sensation of freedom and relief was absolutely delicious. They were like animals escaped from a cage. Moored among the reeds, with the *African Queen* actually rocking a little to a minute swell coming in from the lake, they slept more peacefully, plagued though they were with frogs and flies, than they had for days.

And in the morning there was still no discussion of the torpedoing of the *Königin Luise*. To Rose with her methodical mind it was necessary to complete one step before thinking about the next.

"Let's get the boat cleaned out," she said. "I can't bear all this."

Indeed, in the glaring sunlight the filth and mess in the boat was perfectly horrible. Rose literally could not think or plan, surrounded by such conditions. They jangled her nerves unbearably. No matter if the *African Queen* were shortly to be blown to pieces when she should immolate herself against the *Königin Luise*'s side, Rose could not bear the thought of passing even two or three days unnecessarily in that dirt.

The water overside was clear and clean. By degrees they washed the whole boat, although it involved moving everything from place to place while they washed. Allnutt got the floor boards up and cleaned out the reeking bilge, while Rose knelt up in the sternsheets and gradually worked clean the rugs and the clothing and the articles of domestic utility. It was a splendid day, and in that sunshine even a thick rug dried almost while you looked at it. Such a domestic interlude was the best sort of holiday Rose could have had; perhaps it was not only coincidence that they both missed their attacks of malaria that morning.

Rose got herself clean, too, for the first time since their entry into the mangroves, and felt once more the thrill of putting on a fresh clean frock on a fresh clean body. That was literally the case, because Rose had taken the step which she had tried to put aside in the old days of the mission station — she was wearing no underclothes. Most of them had been consumed in the service of the boat — as hand shields when the propeller shaft was straightened, and so on — and the rest were dedicated to Allnutt's use. His own clothing had disintegrated, and now he moved chastely about the boat in Rose's chemise and drawers; the modest trimming round the neck and the infinite number of tucks about his thighs were in comical contrast with his lean, unfeminine form.

Perhaps it was as a result of these civilized preoccupations that Rose that night thought of something which had slipped from her memory utterly and completely from the moment she had left the mission station. She herself, later, believed on occasions that it was God himself who came and roused her from her sleep, her breast throbbing and the blood pulsing warm under her skin, although when she was in a more modest mood she attributed it to her "better self," or her conscience.

She had not said her prayers since she joined the *African Queen;* she had not even thought about God. She woke with a start as this realization came upon her, and she lay with wave after wave of remorse — and fear, too — sweeping over her. She could not understand how it was that the God she worshipped had not sent the lightning, which had so frequently torn the sky about her, to destroy her. She was in an agony lest He should do so now, before she could appease him. She scrambled up to her knees and clasped her hands, and bowed her head and prayed in a passion of remorse.

Allnutt, waking in the night, saw the profile of her bowed figure in the starlight, and saw her lift her face to heaven with her cheeks wet with tears and her lips moving. He was awed by the sight. He did not pray himself, and never had done so. The fact that Rose was able to pray in tears and agony showed him the superiority of her clay over his. But it was a superiority of which he had long been aware. He was content to leave the appeal for heavenly guidance to Rose, just as he had left to her the negotiation of the rapids of the Ulanga. It took a very great deal to deprive Allnutt of his sleep. His eyes closed and he drifted off again, leaving Rose to bear her agony alone.

In that awful moment Rose would have found no comfort in Allnutt anyway. It was a matter only for her and God. There was no trace of the iron-nerved woman who had brought the *African Queen* down the Ulanga, in the weeping figure who besought God for forgiveness of her neglect. She could make no attempt to compound with God, to offer future good behaviour in exchange for forgiveness of the past, because her training did not permit it. She could only plead utter abject penitence, and beg for forgiveness as an arbitrary favour from the stern God about whom her brother had taught her. She was torn with misery. She could not tell if she were forgiven or not. She did not know how much of hellfire she would have to endure on account of these days of forgetfulness.

Worse still, she could not tell whether her angry God might not see fit to punish her additionally by blasting

her present expedition with failure. It would be an apt
punishment, seeing that the expedition was the cause of
her neglect. There was a biblical flavour about it which
tore her with apprehension. In redoubled agony she
begged and prayed to God to look with favour on this
voyage of the *African Queen,* to grant them an opportunity of finding the *Königin Luise* and of sinking her so
that the hated iron cross flag would disappear from the
waters of Lake Wittelsbach and the allies might pour
across to the conquest of German Central Africa. She was
quite frantic with doubts and fear; the joints of her fingers
cracked with the violence with which she clasped them.

It was only then that she remembered another sin —
a worse one, the worst sin of all in the bleak minds of
those who had taught her, a sin whose name she had only
used when reading aloud from the Bible. She had lain
with a man in unlicensed lust. For a moment she remembered with shocked horror the things she had done with
that man, her wanton immodesty. It made matters worse
still that she had actually *enjoyed* it, as no woman should
ever dream of doing.

She looked down at the vague, white figure of Allnutt
asleep in the bottom of the boat, and with that came reaction. She could not, she absolutely could not, feel a conviction of sin with regard to him. He was as much a
husband to Rose as any married woman's husband was to
her, whatever the formalities with which she and Charlie
had dispensed. She took courage from the notion, although she did not rise (or sink) to the level of actually
wording to herself her opinion of the marriage sacrament

as a formality. She lapsed insensibly into the heresy of be-lieving that it might be possible that natural forces could be too strong for her, and that if they were she was not to blame.

Much of her remorse and terror departed from her in that moment, and she calmed perceptibly. The last of her prayers were delivered with reason as well as feeling, and she asked favours now as one friend might ask of another. The sincerity of her conviction that what she meditated doing on England's behalf must be right came to her res-cue, so that hope and confidence came flooding back again despite the weakness which the first agony had brought to her sick body. There descended upon her at last a certainty of righteousness as immovable and as un-reasoning as her previous conviction of sin.

In the end she lay down again to sleep with her seren-ity quite restored, completely fanatical again about the justice and the certainty of success of the blow she was going to strike for England. The only perceptible differ-ence the whole harrowing experience made in her con-duct was that next morning when she rose she prayed again for a moment, on her knees with her head bowed, while Allnutt fidgeted shyly in the bows. She was her old self again, with level brows and composed features, when she rose from her knees to look round the horizon.

There was something in sight out there, something besides water and reeds and sky and islands. It was not a cloud; it was a smudge of black smoke, and beneath it a white dot. Rose's heart leaped violently in her breast, but she forced composure on herself.

"Charlie," she called, quietly enough. "Come up here. What's *that?*"

One glance was sufficient for Allnutt, as it had been for Rose.

"That's the *Louisa.*"

Partisanship affected Allnutt much as it affects the association football crowds which are constituted of thousands of people just like Allnutt. No words could be bad enough for the other side, just because it happened to be the other side. Although Allnutt had not had a chance to be infected by the propaganda which seethed at that moment in the British press, he became at sight of the *Königin Luise* as validly an anti-German as any plump city clerk over military age.

"Yerss," he said, standing up on the gunwale. "That's the *Louisa* all right. Ther beasts! Ther swine!"

He shook his fist at the white speck.

"Which way are they going?" asked Rose, cutting through his objurgations. Allnutt peered over the water, but before he could announce his decision Rose announced it for him.

"They're coming this way!" she said, and then she forced herself again to stay calm.

"They mustn't see us here," she went on, in a natural tone. "Can we get far enough among the reeds for them not to see us?"

Allnutt was already leaping about the boat, picking things up and putting them down again. It was more of an effort for him to speak calmly.

"They'll see the funnel and the awning," he said, in a

lucid interval. Putting up the funnel and the awning stanchions had been part of the spring cleaning of yesterday.

For answer Rose tore the ragged awning down again
from its supports.

"You've got plenty of time to get the funnel down,"
she said. "They won't be able to see it yet, and the reeds
are between them and us. I'll see about the stanchions.
Give me a screwdriver."

Rose had the sense and presence of mind to realize
that if a ship the size of the *Königin Luise* was only a dot
to them, they must be less than a dot to it.

With the top hamper stowed away, the *African Queen*
had a freeboard of hardly three feet; they would be quite
safe among the reeds unless they were looked for specially — and Rose knew that the Germans would have
no idea that the *African Queen* was on the lake. She
looked up and watched the *Königin Luise* carefully.
She was nearer, coasting steadily southward along the
margin of the lake. From one dot she had grown into
two — her white hull being visible under her high
bridge. It would be fully an hour before she opened up
the mouth of the river and could see the *African Queen*
against the reeds.

"Let's get the boat in now," she said.

They swung her round so that her bows pointed into
the reeds. Pulling and tugging with the boat hooks
against the reed roots they got her halfway in, but all her
stern still projected out into the channel.

"You'll have to cut some of those reeds down. How
deep is the mud?" said Rose.

Allnutt probed the mud about the *African Queen*'s bows and dubiously contemplated the result.

"Hurry up," snapped Rose, testily, and Allnutt took his knife and went over the bows among the reeds. He sank in the mud until the surface water was up to his armpits. Floundering about, he cut every reed within reach as low as he could manage it. Then, holding the bow painter, with Rose's help he was able to pull himself out of the clinging mud, and lay across the foredeck while Rose worked the *African Queen* up into the space he had cleared.

"There's still a bit sticking out," said Rose. "Once more will do it."

Allnutt splashed back among the reeds and went on cutting. When he had finished and climbed on board again, between the two of them they hauled the boat up into the cleared space. The reeds which the bows had thrust aside when they entered began to close again round the stern.

"It would be better if we were a bit farther in still," said Rose, and without a word Allnutt went in among the reeds once more.

This time the gain was sufficient. The *African Queen* lay in thick reeds; about her stern was a thin but satisfactory screen of the reeds at the edge, which, coming back to the vertical, made her safe against anything but close observation even if — as was obviously unlikely — the *Königin Luise* should see fit to come up the reed-bordered channel to the delta.

Standing on the gunwale, Rose and Allnutt could just

see over the reeds. The *Königin Luise* was holding steadily on her course, a full mile from the treacherous shoals of the shore. She was nearly opposite the mouth of the channel now, and she showed no signs of turning. They watched her for five minutes. She looked beautiful in her glittering white paint against the vivid blue of the water. A long pennant streamed from the brief pole mast beside her funnel; at her stern there floated the flag of the Imperial German Navy with its black cross. On her deck in the bows they could just discern the six-pounder gun which gave the Germans the command of Lake Wittelsbach. No Arab dhow, no canoe, could show her nose outside the creeks and inlets of the lake unless the *Königin Luise* gave permission.

She was past the channel now, still keeping rigidly to the south. There was clearly no danger of discovery; she was on a cruise of inspection round the lake, just making certain that there was no furtive flouting of authority. Rose watched her go, and then got down heavily into the sternsheets.

"My malaria's started again," she said, wearily.

Her face was drawn and apprehensive as a result of the ache she had been enduring in her joints, and her teeth were already chattering. Allnutt wrapped her in the rugs and made what preparations he could for the fever which would follow.

"Mine's begun too," he said then. Soon both of them were helpless and shivering, and moaning a little, under the blazing sun.

Chapter 14

WHEN the attack was over in the late afternoon, Rose got uncertainly to her feet again. Allnutt was only now coming out of the deep, reviving sleep which follows the fever of malaria in fortunate persons. The first thing Rose did was what everyone living in a boat comes to do after an unguarded interval. She stood up and looked about her, craning her neck over the reeds so as to sweep the horizon.

Down in the south she saw it again, that smudge of smoke and that white speck. She formed and then discarded the idea that the *Königin Luise* was still holding her old course. The gunboat was returning; she must have cruised down out of sight to the south and then begun to retrace her course. Allnutt came and stood beside her, and without a word they watched the *Königin Luise* gradually grow larger and more distinct as she came back along the coast. It was Allnutt who broke the silence.

"D'you fink she's looking for us?" he asked, hoarsely.

"No," said Rose, with instant decision. "Not at all. She's only keeping guard on the coast."

Rose was influenced more by faith than by judgment. Her mission would be too difficult to succeed if the Germans were on the lookout for them, and therefore it could not be so.

"Hope you're right," said Allnutt. "Matter of fact, I fink you are myself."

"She's going a different way now!" said Rose, suddenly.

The *Königin Luise* had altered her course a trifle, and was standing out from the shore.

"She's not looking for us, then," said Allnutt.

They watched her as she steered across the lake, keeping just above their horizon, heading for the islands which they could see straight opposite them.

"Wonder what she's goin' to do?" said Allnutt, but all the same it was he who first noticed that when she came to a stop.

"She's anchoring there for the night," said Allnutt. "Look!"

The flag at the stern disappeared, as is laid down as a rule to be followed at sunset in the Imperial Instructions for Captains of Ships of the Imperial German Marine.

"Did you 'ear anything then?" asked Allnutt.

"No."

"I fort I 'eard a bugle." Allnutt could not possibly have heard a bugle over four miles of water, not even in the stillness which prevailed, but undoubtedly there were bugles blowing on the *Königin Luise* at approximately that

time. Even though the crew of the *Königin Luise* con-
sisted only of six white officers and twenty-five coloured
ratings, everything was done on board as befitted the exacting standards of the navy of which the ship was a part.

"Well, there they are," said Allnutt. "And there
they'll stop. That's a good anchorage out there among the
islands. We'll see 'em go in the morning."

He got down from the gunwale while Rose yet lingered. The sun had set in a sudden blaze of colour, and it
was almost too dark to see the distant white speck. She
could not accept as philosophically as Allnutt the in-
evitability of their present inaction. They were on the
threshold of events. They must make ready, and plan, and
strike their blow for England, even though any scheme
seemed more fantastic now than when viewed from the
misty distance of the upper Ulanga.

"We ought to have been ready for them today," said
Rose, turning bitterly to Allnutt, the glow of whose cigarette she could just see in the dark.

Allnutt puffed at his cigarette, and then brought out a
surprisingly helpful suggestion.

"Coo," he said, "don't you worry. I been thinking.
They'll come 'ere agine, you just see if they don't. You
know what these Germans are. They lays down systems
and they sticks to 'em. Mondays they're at one plice, Tues-
days they're somewhere else, Wednesdays p'raps, they're
'ere — I dunno what dye it is todye. Saturday nights I
expect they goes in to Port Livingstone an' lays up over
Sunday. Then they start agine on Monday, same ole round.
You know."

Allnutt was without doubt the psychologist of the two. What he said was so much in agreement with what Rose had seen of official German methods that she could not but think there must be truth in it. He went on to press home his point by example.

"Up at the mine," he said, "Old Kaufman, the inspector, 'oo 'ad the job of seeing that the mine was being run right — an' a fat lot o' good all those rules of theirs was, too — 'e used to turn up once a week regular as clockwork. Always knew when 'e was coming, the Belgians did, an' they'd 'ave everything ready for 'im. 'E'd come in an' look round, and 'ave a drink, an' then off 'e'd go agine wiv 'is Askaris an' 'is bearers. Used to mike me laugh even then."

"Yes, I remember," said Rose, absently. She could remember how Samuel had sometimes chafed against the woodenness of German rules and routine. There could be no doubt that if the *Königin Luise* had once moored amongst these islands she would do so again. Then — her plan was already formed.

"Charlie," she said, and her voice was gentle.

"Yerss, old girl?"

"You must start getting those torpedoes ready. Tomorrow morning, as soon as it's light. How long will it take?"

"I can get the stuff into the tubes in no time, as you might say. Dunno about the detonators. Got to mike 'em, you see. Might take a coupler dyes easy. Matter of fact, I 'aven't thought about 'em prop'ly. Then we got to cut those 'oles in the bows — that won't tike long. Might 'ave

it all done in a coupler dyes. Everything. If we don't 'ave
malaria too bad. Depends on them detonators."

"All right." There was something unnatural about
Rose's voice.

"Rosie, old girl," said Allnutt. "Rosie."

"Yes, dear?"

"I know what you're thinkin' about doing. You
needn't try to 'ide it from me."

Had it not been for the discordant cockney accent
Allnutt's voice in its gentleness might have been that of
some actor in a sentimental moment on the stage. He
took her hand in the darkness and pressed it, unrespon-
sive as it was.

"Not now, you needn't 'ide it, darling," he said. Even
at that moment his cockney self-consciousness came to
embarrass him, and he tried to keep the emotion out of
his voice. For them there was neither the unrestraint of
primitive people nor the acquired self-control of other
classes of society.

"You want to tike the *African Queen* out at night next
time the *Louisa*'s 'ere, don't yer, old girl?" said Allnutt.

"Yes."

"I fink it's the best chance we got of all," said Allnutt.
"We oughter manage it."

Allnutt was silent for a second or two, making ready
for his next argument. Then he spoke.

"You needn't come, old girl. There ain't no need for
us both to — to do it. I can manage it meself, easy."

"Of course not," said Rose. "That wouldn't be fair.

It's you who ought to stay behind. I can manage the launch on my own as far as those islands. That's what I was meaning to do."

"I know," said Allnutt, surprisingly. "But it's me that ought to do it. Besides, with them beggars —"

It was an odd argument that developed. Allnutt was perfectly prepared by now to throw away the life that had seemed so precious to him. This plan of Rose's which had already materialized so far and so surprisingly had become like a living thing to him — like a piece of machinery, would perhaps be a better analogy in Allnutt's case. There would be something wrong about leaving it incomplete. And somehow the sight of the *Königin Luise* cruising about the lake "as bold as brass" had irritated Allnutt. He was aflame with partisanship. He was ready for any mad sacrifice which would upset those beggars' apple cart — presumably Allnutt's contact with the German nation had been unfortunate; the Germans were a race it was easy to hate if hatred came easily, as it did in those days. There was a fierce recklessness about him in odd contrast with his earlier cowardice.

Perhaps no one can really understand the state of mind of a man who volunteers in war for duty that may lead to death, but that such volunteers are always forthcoming has been proved by too many pitiful events in history.

Allnutt tried to reason with Rose. Although they had both of them tacitly dropped their earlier plan of sending the *African Queen* out on her last voyage with no crew on board — Rose knew too much about the launch's little ways by now — Allnutt tried to argue that for him there would be no serious risk. He could dive off the stern of the boat a second before the crash, as soon as he was sure that she would attain the target. Even if he were at the tiller (as privately he meant to be, to make certain), the explosion right up in the bows might not hurt him — Allnutt had the nerve to suggest that even when he had a very sound knowledge of the power of explosives and could guess fairly accurately what two hundredweight of high explosive would do if it went off all at once. In fact, Allnutt was on the point of arguing that blowing up the *Königin Luise* would be a perfectly safe proceeding for anybody, until he saw what a loophole that would leave for Rose's argument.

It all ended, as was inevitable, in their agreeing in the end that they would both go. There was no denying that their best chance of success lay in having one person to steer and one to tend the engine. It was further agreed between them that when they were fifty yards from the *Königin Luise* one of them would jump overboard with the life buoy; but Allnutt thought that it was settled that Rose should do the jumping, and Rose thought that it would be Allnutt.

"Not more'n a week from now," said Allnutt, meditatively.

They had a feeling of anticipation which if not exactly pleasurable was not really unpleasant. They had been working like slaves for weeks now at imminent risk of their lives to this one end, and they had grown so obsessed with the idea that they could not willingly contemplate any action which might imperil its consummation. And in Rose there burned the flame of fanatical patriotism as well. She was so convinced of the rightness of the action she contemplated, and of the necessity for it, that other considerations — even Charlie's safety — weighed with her hardly at all. She could reconcile herself to Charlie's peril as she might have reconciled herself if he were seriously ill, as something quite necessary and unavoidable. The conquest of German Central Africa was vastly, immeasurably more important than their own welfare — so immeasurably more important that it never occurred to her to weigh the one against the other. She glowed, she actually felt a hot flush, when she thought of the triumph of England.

She rose in the darkness, with Allnutt beside her, and looked over the vague reeds across the lake. There were stars overhead, and stars faintly reflected in the water. The moon had not yet risen. But right over there, there was a bundle of faint lights which were neither stars nor their reflections. She clasped Allnutt's arm.

"That's them, all right," said Allnutt.

Rose only realized then what a practical sailor would have thought of long before, that if the Germans took the precaution of biding all lights when they were anchored the task of finding them on a dark night might well be impossible. Yet as they were in the only ship on the lake, and forty miles from their nearest earthbound enemy, there was obviously no need for precaution.

The sight of those lights made their success absolutely

certain, at the moment when Rose first realized that it might have not been quite so certain. She felt a warm gratitude towards the fate which had been so kind. It was in wild exaltation that she clasped Allnutt's arm. In all the uncertainty of future peril and all the certainty of future triumph she clung to him in overwhelming passion. Her love for him and her passion for her country were blended inextricably, strangely. She kissed him in the starlight as Joan of Arc might have kissed a holy relic.

Chapter 15

IN the morning they saw the *Königin Luise* get under way and steam off to the northward again on her interminable patrolling of the lake.

"We'll be ready for her when she comes back," said Rose, tensely.

"Yerss," said Allnutt.

With Rose's help he extricated the two heavy gas cylinders from the bottom of the boat and slid them back handily to the waist. They were foul with rust, but so thick was the steel that they could have borne months more of such exposure without weakening. Allnutt turned on the taps, and all the air was filled with an explosive hissing, as the gas poured out and the pressure gauge needles moved slowly back to zero. When the hissing had subsided Allnutt got to work with his tools and extracted the whole nose-fitting from each cylinder There was left a round blank hole in each, opening into the empty dark within.

Very carefully they prized open the boxes of explosive. They were packed with what looked like fat candles of pale yellow wax, each wrapped in oiled paper. Allnutt began methodically and cautiously to pack the cylinders with them, putting his arm far down into the interior.

"M'm," said Allnutt. "It'd be better if they weren't loose like this."

He looked around the boat for packing material, and was momentarily at a loss. His ingenuity had been sharpened by all the recent necessity to employ makeshifts.

"Mud's the stuff," he announced.

He went up into the bows and, leaning over the side, he began to scoop up handfuls of the black mud from the bottom, and slapped them down upon the foredeck to become nearly dry in the sun.

"I'll do that," said Rose, as soon as she realized what he intended.

She squeezed the water from the stinking black mud, and then spread the handfuls on the hot deck, and worked upon them until they were nearly hard. Then she carried the sticky mass back to Allnutt and set herself to preparing more.

Bit by bit Allnutt filled the cylinders, cementing each layer of explosive hard and firm with mud. When each was full right up to the neck he stood up to ease his aching back.

"That's done prop'ly," he said with pride, looking down at the results of his morning's work, and Rose nodded approval, contemplating the deadly things lying on the floor boards. Neither of them saw anything in the least fantastic in the situation.

"We got to make them detonators now," he said. "I got an idea. Thought of it last night."

From the locker in which his toilet things were stored he brought out a revolver, heavily greased to preserve it from the air. Rose stared at the thing in amazement; it was the first she knew of the presence of such a weapon in the boat.

"I 'ad to 'ave this," explained Allnutt. "I used to 'ave a lot o' gold on board 'ere going up to Limbasi sometimes. A nundred ounces an' more, some weeks. I never 'ad to shoot nobody, though."

"I'm glad you didn't," said Rose. To shoot a thief in time of peace seemed a much more unpleasant thing than to blow up a whole ship in time of war.

Allnutt broke open the revolver and took the cartridges into his hand, replacing the empty revolver in the locker.

"Now let me see," he said, musingly.

Rose watched the idea gradually taking shape under his hands; the things took time to construct — what with meals and sleep and malaria, it was all of the two days of Allnutt's previous rough estimate before they were ready.

First he had, very laboriously, to shape with his knife two round discs of hard wood which would screw tightly into the noses of the cylinders. Then in each disc he pierced three holes of such a size that he could just force the cartridges into them. When the discs were in position in the nozzles, the bullets and the ends of the brass cartridge cases would now rest in among the explosive.

The rest of the work was far more niggling and delicate, and Allnutt discarded several pieces before he was satisfied. He cut two more discs of wood of the same size as the previous two, and he was meticulous about what sort of wood he used. He wanted it neither hard nor rotten, something through which a nail could be driven as easily as possible and yet which would hold the nail firmly without allowing it to wobble. He made several experiments in driving nails into the various kinds of wood at his disposal before he eventually decided to use a piece of one of the floor boards.

Rose quite failed to guess at the motive of these experiments, but she was content to sit and watch, and hand things to him, as he worked away in the flaming sunlight, the masses of mosquitoes always about him.

When the new discs were cut, Allnutt carefully laid them on the others and noted exactly where the bases of the cartridges would rest against them. At these points he made ready to drive nails through the new discs, and, as a final meticulous precaution, he filed the points of the nails to the maximum of sharpness. He drove the nails gingerly through the discs at the points which he had marked, and on the other side he pared away small circles of wood into which the bases of the cartridges would fit exactly, so when that was done the points of the nails were just showing as gleaming traces of metal in the middle of each shallow depression, while on the other side the heads of the nails protruded for a full inch.

Finally, he screwed his pairs of discs together.

"That's all right now," said Allnutt.

Each pair of discs was now one disc. On one side of the disc showed the nailheads, whose points rested against the percussion caps in the bases of the cartridges, the bullets of which showed on the opposite side. It was easy to see now that when the disc was in its place in the cylinder nose, and the cylinder pointing beyond the bows of the *African Queen,* the boat would be herself a locomotive torpedo. When she was driven at full speed against the side of a ship the nails would be struck sharply against the cartridges. They would explode into the high explosive packed tight in the cylinders.

"I don't think I could do it any better," said Allnutt, half apologetically. "They ought to work all right."

There were three cartridges to each cylinder; one at least ought to explode; and there were two cylinders, each containing nearly a hundredweight of explosive — one cylinder, let alone two, ought to settle a little ship like the *Königin Luise.*

"Yes," said Rose, with all the gravity the situation demanded. "They ought to work all right."

They had all the seriousness of children discussing the construction of a sand castle.

"Can't put 'em into the cylinders yet," explained Allnutt. "They're a bit tricky. We better get the cylinders into position now an' leave the detonators till last. We can put 'em in when we're all ready to start. After we got out of these reeds."

"Yes," said Rose. "It'll be dark, then, of course. Will you be able to do it in the dark?"

"It's a case of 'ave to," said Allnutt. "Yerss, I can do it all right."

Rose formed a mental picture of their starting out; it certainly would be risky to try to push the *African Queen* out from the reeds in the darkness with two torpedoes which would explode at a touch protruding from the bow.

Allnutt put the detonators away in the locker with the utmost care, and turned to think out the remainder of the preparations necessary.

"We want to 'ave the explosion right down low," he said. "Can't 'ave it too low. Fink it's best to make those 'oles for the cylinders."

It was a toilsome, back-breaking job, although it called for no particular skill, to cut two holes, one each side of the stem, in the *African Queen*'s bows, just above the water line. When they were finished, Rose and All-nutt dragged and pushed the cylinders forward until their noses were well through the holes, a good foot in front of any part of the boat. Allnutt stuffed the ragged edges with chips of wood and rags.

"Doesn't matter if it leaks a little," he said. "It's only splashes which'll be coming in, 'cause the bow rides up when we're going along. All we got to do now is to fix them cylinders down tight."

He nailed them solidly into position with battens split from the cases of provisions, adding batten to batten and piling all the available loose gear on top to make quite sure. The more those cylinders were confined the more effective would be their explosion against the side of the *Königin Luise*. When the last thing was added Allnutt sat down.

"Well, old girl," he said, "we done it all now. Everything. We're all ready."

It was a solemn moment. The consummation of all their efforts, their descent of the rapids of the Ulanga, their running the gauntlet at Shona, the mending of the propeller, their toil in the water-lily pool and their agony in the delta, was at hand.

"Coo," said Allnutt, reminiscently, " 'aven't we just 'ad a time! Been a regular bank 'oliday."

Rose forgave him his irreverence.

As a result of having completed the work so speedily, they now had to endure the strain of waiting. They were idle now for the first time since the dreadful occasion — which they were both so anxious to forget — when Rose had refused to speak to Allnutt. From that time they had been ceaselessly busy; they had an odd empty feeling when they contemplated the blank days ahead of them, even though they were to be their last days on earth.

Those last days were rather terrible. There was one frightening interval when Allnutt felt his resolution waver. He felt like a man in a condemned cell waiting for the last few days before his execution to expire. As a young man in England he had often read about that, in the ghoulish Sunday newspaper which had constituted his only reading. Somehow it was his memory of what he had read which frightened him, not the thought of the imminent explosion — it deprived him of his new-won manhood and took him back into his pulpy youth, so that he clung to Rose with a new urgency, and she, marvelously, understood, and soothed him and comforted him.

The sun glared down upon them pitilessly; they were without even the shelter of the awning, which might betray them if it showed above the reeds. Every hour was pregnant with monotony and weariness; there was always the lurking danger that they might come to hate each other, crouching there among the reeds as in a grave. They felt that danger, and they fought against it.

Even the thunderstorms were a relief; they came with black clouds, and a mighty breath of wind which whipped the lake into fury so that they could hear breakers roar upon the shoals, and the whole lake was covered with tossing white horses, until even in their reedy sanctuary the violence of the water reached them, so that the *African Queen* heaved uneasily and sluggishly under them.

To pass away the time they overhauled the engine thoroughly, so as to make quite certain that it would function properly on its last run. Allnutt wallowed in the mud beneath the boat and ascertained by touch that the propeller and shaft were as sound as they could be hoped to be. Every few minutes throughout every day, one or the other of them climbed on the gunwale and looked out over the reeds across the Lake, scanning the horizon for sight of the *Königin Luise*. They saw a couple of dhows — or it may have been the same one twice — sailing down what was evidently the main passage through the islands, but that was all the sign of life they saw for some days. They even came to doubt whether the *Königin Luise* would ever appear again in her previous anchorage. They had grown unaccustomed to counting the passage of time, and they actually were not sure how many days had lapsed since they saw her last. Even after the most careful counting back they could not come to an agreement on the point, and they began to eye each other regretfully and wonder whether they had not better issue forth from their hiding place and coast along the edge of the lake in search of their victim. In black moments they began to doubt whether they would ever achieve their object.

Until one morning they looked out over the reeds and saw her just as before, a smudge of smoke and a white dot, coming down from the north. Just as before she steamed steadily by to the south and vanished below their low horizon, and the hours crawled by painfully until the afternoon revealed her smoke again returning, and they were sure she would anchor again among the islands. Allnutt had been nearly right in his guess about the methodical habits of the Germans. In their careful patrolling of the lake they never omitted a periodical cruise into this, the most desolate corner of the Wittelsbach Nyanza, just to see that all was well, even though the forbidding marshes of the Bora delta and the wild forests beyond made it unlikely that any menace to the German command of the lake could develop here.

Allnutt and Rose watched the *Königin Luise* come back from her excursion to the south, and they saw her head over towards the islands, and, as the day was wan-ing, they saw her come to a stop at the point where she had anchored before. Both their hearts were beating faster. It was then that the question they had debated in academic fashion a week earlier without reaching a satisfactory conclusion solved itself. They had just turned away from looking at the *Königin Luise,* about to make preparations to start, when they found themselves holding each other's hands and looking into each other's eyes. Each of them knew what was in the other's mind.

"Rosie, old girl," said Allnutt, hoarsely. "We're going out *together,* aren't we?"

Rose nodded.

"Yes, dear," she said. "I should like it that way."

Confronted with the sternest need for a decision, she had reached it without difficulty. They would share all the dangers, and stand the same chance, side by side, when the *African Queen* drove her torpedoes smashing against the side of the *Königin Luise.* They could not endure the thought of being parted, now. They could even smile at the prospect of going into eternity together.

It was almost dark by now. The young moon was low in the sky; soon there would only be the stars to give them light.

"It's safe for us to get ready now," said Rose. "Goodbye, dear."

"Goodbye darling, sweet'eart," said Allnutt.

Their preparations took much time, as they had anticipated. They had all night before them, and they knew that as it was a question of surprise the best time they could reach the *Königin Luise* would be in the early hours of the morning. Allnutt had to go down into the mud and water and cut away the reeds about the *African Queen*'s stern before they could slide her out into the channel again — the reeds which had parted before her bows resisted obstinately the passage of her stern and propeller.

When they were in the river, moored lightly to a great bundle of reeds, Allnutt quietly took the detonators from the locker and went into the water again over the bows. He was a long time there, standing in mud and deep water while he screwed the detonators home into the noses of the cylinders. The rough-and-ready screw threads he had scratched in the edges of his discs did not enter kindly into their functions. Allnutt had to use force, and it was a slow process to use force in the dark on a detonator in contact with a hundredweight of high explosive. Rose stood in the bows to help him at need as he worked patiently at the task. If his hand should slip against those nailheads they would be blown into fragments, and the *Königin Luise* would still rule the waves of the lake.

Nor did the fact that the *African Queen* was pitching a little in a slight swell coming in from the lake help Allnutt at all in his task, but he finished it in the end. In the almost pitch dark, Rose saw him back away from the torpedoes and come round at a safe distance to the side of the boat. His hands reached up and he swung himself on board, dripping.

"Done it," he whispered — they could not help whispering in that darkness with the obsession of their future errand upon them.

Allnutt groped about the boat putting up the funnel

again. He made a faint noise with his spanner as he tightened up the nuts on the funnel stay bolts. It all took time.

The furnace was already charged with fuel — that much, at any rate, they had been able to make ready days ago — and the tin canister of matches was in its right place, and he could light the dry friable stuff and close down to force the draught. He knew just whereabouts to lay his hands on the various sorts of wood he might need before they reached the *Königin Luise.*

There was a wind blowing now, and the *African Queen* was very definitely pitching to the motion of the water. The noise of the draught seemed loud to their anxious ears, and when Allnutt recharged the furnace a volley of sparks shot from the funnel and was swept away overhead. Rose had never seen sparks issue from that funnel before — she had only been in the *African Queen* under way in daylight — and she realized the danger that the sparks might reveal their approach. She spoke quietly to Allnutt about it.

"Can't 'elp it, Miss, sometimes," he whispered back. "I'll see it don't 'appen when we're getting close to 'em."

The engine was sighing and slobbering now; if it had been daylight they would have seen the steam oozing out of the leaky joints.

"S'ss, s'ss," whistled Allnutt, between his teeth.

"All right," said Rose.

Allnutt unfastened the side painter and took the boat hook. A good thrust against a clump of reeds sent the boat out into the fairway; he laid the boat hook down, and felt for the throttle valve and opened it. The propeller began its beat and the engine its muffled clanking. Rose stood at the tiller and steered out down the dark river mouth. They were off now, to strike their blow for the land of hope and glory of which Rose had sung as a child at concerts in Sunday school choirs. They were going to set wider those bounds and make the mighty country mightier yet.

The *African Queen* issued forth upon the lake to gain which they had run such dangers and undergone such toil. Out through her bows pointed the torpedoes, two hundredweight of explosive which a touch could set off. Down by the engine crouched Allnutt, his whole attention concentrated on ascertaining by ear what he had been accustomed to judge by sight — steam pressure and water level and lubrication. Rose stood in the tossing stern, and her straining eyes could just see the tiny light which marked the presence of the *Königin Luise;* there were no stars overhead.

If it had been daylight they would have marked the banking up of the clouds overhead, the tense stickiness of the electricity-charged atmosphere. If they had been experienced in lake conditions they would have known what that ominous wind foretold; they had no knowledge of the incredible speed with which the wind, whipping down from the mountains of the north, roused the shallow waters of the lake to maniacal fury.

Rose had had her training in rivers; it did not occur to her to look for danger where there were no rocks, nor weeds, nor rapids. When in the darkness the *African Queen* began to pitch and wallow in rough water she cared nothing for it. She felt no appreciation of the fact that the shallow-draught launch was not constructed to encounter rough water, and that she was out of reach of land now in a boat whose wall sides and flat bottom made her the least unseaworthy vessel it is possible to imagine. She found it difficult to keep her feet as the *African Queen* swayed and staggered about in haphazard fashion. In the darkness there was no way of anticipating her extravagant rolling. Waves were crashing against the flat sides; the tops of them were coming in over the edge, but that sort of thing was, in Rose's mind, only to be expected in open water. She had no fear at all.

The wind seemed to have dropped for a moment, but the water was still rough. Then suddenly the darkness was torn away for a second by a dazzling flash of lightning which revealed the wild water round them, and the thunder followed with a single loud bang like a thousand cannons fired at once. Then came the rain, pouring down through the blackness in solid rivers, numbing and stupefying, and with the rain came the wind, suddenly, from a fresh quarter, laying its grip on the torn surface of the lake and heaving it up into mountains, while the lightning still flashed and the thunder bellowed in madness. With the shift of the wind the *African Queen* began to pound, heaving her bows out of the water and bringing them down again with a shattering crash. It was as well that Allnutt had selected the type of fuse he had employed;

any other might have been touched off by the pounding waves, but the water which could toss about a two-ton boat like a toy could not drive nails.

It was all dark; Rose had no way of knowing if the stupefying water which was deluging her was rain or spray or waves. In that chaos all she could do was to keep her hand on the tiller and try to keep her footing. There was no possible chance of seeing the lights of the *Königin Luise.*

Allnutt was at her side. He was putting her arm through the huge lumbering life buoy which had always seemed to bulk so unnecessarily large in the boat's equipment. Then as they tottered and swayed in the drenching dark, he was taken from her. She tried to call to him unavailingly. She felt a surge of cold water round her waist. A wave smacked her in the face; she was strangling with the water in her nostrils.

The *African Queen* had sunk, and with her ended the gallant attempt to torpedo the *Königin Luise* for England's sake. And, as though the storm had been raised just for Germany's benefit, it died away with the sinking of the *African Queen,* and the wayward water fell smooth again, just as it had done once long ago on another inland sea, that of Galilee.

Chapter 16

∽∽∽

THE President of the Court looked with curiosity at the prisoner. He tried conscientiously not to see him as he was now, but as he might have looked in civilized array. He tried to discount the mop of long, tangled hair, and the sprouting beard, and he told himself that it was an ordinary face, one that might pass quite unnoticed on the Kurfürstendamm any day of the week. The prisoner was a sick man. That was obvious additionally to his weary and disheartened manner, and his feebleness was due to illness as well as to fatigue. The President of the Court told himself that if ever he had seen the characteristic features of malaria he saw them now in the prisoner.

The rags he was dressed in added to the drama of his appearance — and here the President suddenly leaned forward (the shoulders of his tunic had stuck to the back of his chair with sweat) and he looked with greater attention. The ragged singlet the man was wearing had some

kind of tattered frilling at the throat. His breeches had
frills and tucks, ragged but recognizable. The President
sat back in his chair again; the man was wearing a
woman's underclothing. That made the case more interesting; he might be mad, or — whatever it was, it was not
the simple case of spying he had anticipated. There might
be something in his defence.

The prosecuting officer stated the case against the
prisoner; there must be due regard to formalities, even
though it involved telling the Court facts which were
perfectly well known to it. The prisoner had been seen
on the island of Prinz Eitel, at dawn, and, having been
promptly hunted down and arrested, could give no account of himself. The Court was aware of this, seeing that
it had been the President of the Court who had observed
him from the deck of the *Königin Luise,* and the other
member of the Court who had questioned him.

The prosecuting officer pointed out that on the island
were kept reserve stores of fuel for the *Königin Luise,*
which an evilly disposed person might easily destroy; this
was additional to the fact that the island offered unri-
valled opportunities for spying upon the movements of
the *Königin Luise.* And it was hardly necessary to press
these points, because the prisoner was obviously an alien,
and he had been found in an area prohibited to all but
members of the forces of His Imperial Majesty the Kaiser
and King, by a proclamation of His Excellency General
Baron Von Hanneken, and so he was liable to the death
penalty. The prosecuting officer made the quite unneces-

sary addition that a court of two officers, such as the one he was addressing, was perfectly competent to award a penalty of death for espionage in a field court martial.

This peroration annoyed the President; it was almost impertinence on the part of a mere lieutenant to tell a commander what was the extent of his powers. He knew them already; it was by his orders that the Court had constituted itself. The man would be giving him the information that he was the captain of the *Königin Luise* next, and similar irrelevancies. The President turned to the officer charged with the defence.

But Lieutenant Schumann was rather at a loss. He was not a very intelligent officer, but he was the only one available. Of the *Königin Luise*'s six officers, one was watch-keeping on deck, and one in the engine room, two constituted the Court, one was prosecuting, and only old Schumann was left for the defence. He uttered a few halting words, and stopped, tongue-tied. He was shy when it came to public speaking. The President of the Court looked inquiringly at the prisoner.

Allnutt was too dazed and weary and ill to take much note of his surroundings. He was aware in a way that he was being subjected to some sort of trial — the attitude of the two officers in their white suits with the gold braid and buttons told him that — but he was not specifically aware of the charges against him, or of the penalty which might be inflicted. He would not have cared very much anyway. Nothing mattered much now, now that he had lost Rosie and the old *African Queen* was sunk and the great endeavour was at an end. He was ill, and he almost wished he was dead.

He looked up at the President of the Court, and his eyes drifted round to the prosecuting officer and the defending officer. Clearly they were expecting him to say something. It was too much trouble, and they could not understand him, anyway. He looked down at the floor again, and swayed a little on his feet.

The President of the Court knew that it was his duty, failing any one else, to ascertain anything in the accused's favour. He leant forward and tapped the table sharply with his pencil.

"What is your nationality?" he asked in German.

Allnutt looked at him stupidly.

"Belgian?" asked the President. "English?"

At the word *"Englisch"* Allnutt nodded.

"English," he said. "British."

"Your name?" asked the President in German, and then, doing his best to remember his English, he repeated the question.

"Charles Allnutt."

It took a long time to get that down correctly, translating the English names of the letters into German ones.

"What — did — you — on — ve — ve — *Insel?*" asked the President. He could not be surprised when the prisoner did not understand him. By a sudden stroke of genius he realized that the man might speak Swahili, the universal lingua franca of East and Central Africa, half Bantu, half Arabic, the same language as he used to his native sailors. He asked the question again in Swahili, and he saw a gleam of understanding in the prisoner's face. Then instantly he assumed a mask of sullen stupidity again. The President of the Court asked again in Swahili what the prisoner was doing on the island.

"Nothing," said Allnutt sullenly. He was not going to own up to the affair of the *African Queen;* he thought, anyway, that it was wiser not to do so.

"Nothing," he said again in reply to a fresh question.

The President of the Court sighed a little. He would have to pass sentence of death, he could see. He had already done so once since the outbreak of hostilities, and the wretched Arab half-caste had at his orders swung on a gallows at the lakeside as a deterrent to other spies — but bodies did not last long in this climate.

At that moment there was a bustle outside the tiny, crowded cabin. The door opened, and a coloured petty officer came in, dragging with him a fresh prisoner. At sight of her the President rose to his feet, stooping under the low deck, for the prisoner was a woman, and obviously a white woman despite her deep tan. There was a tangled mass of chestnut hair about her face, and she wore only a single garment, which, torn open at the bosom, revealed breasts which made the President feel uneasy.

The petty officer explained that they had found the woman on another of the islands, and, with her, something else. He swung into view a life buoy, and on the life buoy they could see the name *African Queen.*

"*African Queen!*" said the President to himself, raking back in his memory for something half-forgotten.

He opened the drawer in his table, and searched through a mass of papers until he found what he sought. It was a duplicate of the notice sent by Von Hanneken to the captain of reserve. Until that moment the news of a missing steam launch on the Upper Ulanga had had no interest at all for the captain of the *Königin Luise,* but now it was different. He looked at the female prisoner, and his awkwardness about that exposed body returned. She, too, was trying to hold the rags about her. The captain gave a short order to the prosecuting officer, who rose and opened a locker — the cabin in which they were was wardroom and cabin for three officers together — and produced a white uniform jacket, into which he proceeded to help Rose. The making of the gesture produced a reflex of courtesy and deference in the men; with just the same gesture they had helped women into their opera cloaks.

"A chair," said the captain, and the defending officer hastened to proffer his.

"Get out," said the captain to the coloured ratings, and they withdrew, making a good deal more room in the stifling cabin.

"And now, gracious lady," said the captain to Rose. Already he had guessed much. These two people must be the mechanic and the missionary's sister; presumably they had abandoned their launch on the Upper Ulanga and had come down in a canoe, and had been wrecked in last night's storm when trying to cross the lake to the Belgian Congo. He began to question Rose in Swahili; it was an enormous relief to find, from her use of the German variants of that language, that she actually knew a little German — those weary days spent with grammar book and vocabulary under Samuel's sarcastic tutorship were bearing fruit at last.

It was far more of a surprise when it came out that Allnutt and Rose had brought the *African Queen* down the rapids of the Ulanga and through the Bora delta.

"But, gracious lady . . ." protested the captain.

There could be no doubting her statement, all the same. The captain looked at Rose and marvelled. He had heard from Spengler's own lips an account of the rapids and the delta.

"It was very dangerous," said the captain.

Rose shrugged her shoulders. It did not matter. Nothing mattered now. Although she had been glad to see him in the cabin, even her love for Allnutt seemed to be dead, now that the *African Queen* was lost and the *Königin Luise* still ruled the lake.

The captain had heard about the stoicism and ability of Englishwomen; here was a clear proof.

Anyway, there could be no question now of espionage and the death penalty. He could not hang one person without the other, and he never thought for a moment of hanging Rose. He would not have done so even if he thought her guilty; white women were so rare in Central Africa that he would have thought it monstrous. Beyond all else, she had brought a steam launch from the Upper Ulanga to the lake, and that was a feat for which he could feel professional admiration. He gazed at her and marvelled.

"But why," he asked, "did not your friend here tell us?"

Rose looked round at Allnutt, and became conscious of his sick weariness as he still stood, swaying. All her instincts were aroused now. She got up from her chair and went to him protectively.

"He is ill and tired," she said, and then, with indignation, "He ought to be in bed."

Allnutt drooped against her, while she struggled to say in German and Swahili just what she thought of men who could treat a poor creature thus. She stroked his bristly face and murmured endearments to him. In the white uniform jacket and tattered dress she made a fine figure, despite the ravages of malaria.

"But you, madam," said the captain. "You are ill, too."

Rose did not bother to answer him.

The captain looked round the cabin.

"The Court is dismissed," he snapped.

His colleague and the prosecuting officer and the defending officer leaped up to their feet and saluted. They filed out of the cabin while the captain tapped on the table meditatively with his pencil and decided on his future action. These two ought of course to be interned; that was what Von Hanneken would do if he took them into the mainland. But they were ill, and they might die in imprisonment. It was not right that two people who had achieved so much should die in an enemy's hands. All the laws of chivalry dictated that he should do more than that for them. In German Central Africa there would be small comfort for captured enemy civilians. And what differ-

ence would one sick man and one sick woman make to
the balance of a war between two nations?

Von Hanneken would curse when he knew, but after
all the captain of the *Königin Luise* was his own master
on the lake and could do what he liked in his own ship.
The captain formed his resolve almost before the blundering Schumann had closed the cabin door.

Chapter 17

⚯⚯⚯

THE post of Senior Naval Officer, Port Albert, Belgian Congo, was of very new creation. It was only the night before that it had come into being. It was a chance of war that the senior naval officer in a Belgian port should be an English lieutenant-commander. He was standing pacing along the jetty inspecting the preparation for sea of the squadron under his command. Seeing that it comprised only two small motor boats, it seemed a dignified name for it. But those motor boats had cost in blood and sweat and treasure more than destroyers might have done, for they had been sent out from England, and had been brought with incredible effort overland through jungles, by rail and by river, to the harbour in which they lay.

They were thirty-knot boats, and in their bows each would have — when the mounting was completed — an automatic three-pounder gun. Thirty knots and those guns would make short work of the *Königin Luise* with her maximum of nine knots and her old-fashioned six-pounder. The lieutenant-commander paced the jetty impatiently; he was anxious to get to work now that the weary task of transport was completed. It was irksome that there should remain a scrap of water on which the White Ensign did not reign supreme. The sooner they came out on the hunt for the *Königin Luise* the better. He gazed out over the lake and stopped suddenly. There was smoke on the horizon, and below it a white dot. As he looked, a lieutenant came running along the jetty to him; he had binoculars in his hand.

"That's the *Königin Luise* in sight, sir," he said breathlessly, and offered the glasses.

The lieutenant-commander stared through them at the approaching vessel.

"She's nearly hull up from the artillery observing station, sir," said the lieutenant.

"M'm," said the lieutenant-commander, and looked again.

"She looks as if she's expecting action from the number of flags she's got flying," he said. "M'm — half a minute. That's not a German ens'n on the foremast. It's — what do you make of it?"

The lieutenant looked through the glasses in his turn.

"I think . . ." he said, and looked again.

"It's a white flag," he said at last.

"I think so too," said the lieutenant-commander, and the two officers looked at each other.

They had both of them heard stories — which in later

years they would be sorry that they had believed — about the misuse of the white flag by the Germans.

"Wonder what they're after," mused the lieutenant-commander. "Perhaps . . ."

There was no need for him to explain, even if there were time. If the Germans had heard of the arrival of the motor boats on the lake shore they had one last chance to maintain their command of the lake waters. A bold attack — for which a white flag might afford admirable cover — a couple of well-placed shells, and the *Königin Luise* could resume her unchallenged patrol of the lake. The lieutenant-commander ran as fast as his legs would carry him along the jetty and up the slope to the artillery observing station. The Belgian artillery captain was there with his field-glasses; below him in concealed emplacements were the two mountain guns which guarded the port.

"If they're up to any monkey tricks," said the lieutenant-commander, "they'll catch it hot. I can lay one of those mountain guns even if these Belgians can't."

But the Germans had apparently no monkey tricks in mind. The lieutenant-commander had hardly finished speaking before the *Königin Luise* rounded to, broadside on to the shore, far out of range of her six-pounder. The officers in the observing station saw a puff of white smoke from her bow, and the report of a gun came slowly over to them. They saw the white flag at the foremast come down halfway, and then mount again to the masthead.

"That means they want a parley," said the lieutenant-commander; he had never used the word "parley" before in his life, but it was the only one which suited the occasion.

"I'll go," decided the lieutenant-commander. It was not his way to send others on dangerous duties, and there might be danger here, white flag or no white flag.

"You stay here," went on the lieutenant-commander to the lieutenant. "You're in command while I'm out there. If you see any need to fire, fire like blazes — don't mind about me. Understand?"

The lieutenant nodded.

"I'll have to go in one of those dhows," decided the lieutenant-commander, indicating the little cluster of native boats at the far end of the jetty, where they had lain for months for fear of the *Königin Luise,* and where they now screened the activity round the motor boats. He stopped to sort his French sentences out.

"Mon capitaine," he began, addressing the Belgian captain, *"voulez-vous . . ."*

There is no need to describe the lieutenant-commander's linguistic achievements.

The lieutenant watched through his glasses as the dhow headed out from shore with a native crew. The lieutenant-commander in the stern had taken the precaution of changing his jacket for one of plain white drill. The lieutenant watched him steer towards the gunboat, far out on the lake, and in appearance just like a white-painted Thames tug. Soon the yellow sail was all he could see of the dhow; he saw it reach the gunboat, and vanish as it was furled when the dhow ran alongside. There was an anxious delay. Then at last the dhow's sail reappeared; she was coming back. There came another puff of smoke as the *Königin Luise* fired a parting salute, and then she turned away and headed back again towards the invisible German shore. The whole scene had a touch of the formal chivalry of the Napoleonic wars.

When the *Königin Luise* was hull down over the horizon and the dhow was close in-shore the lieutenant left his post and went down to the jetty to meet his senior officer. The dhow ran briskly in, and the native crew furled the sail as she slid alongside the jetty. The lieutenant-commander was there in the stern-sheets. Lying in the bottom of the boat were two new passengers, at whom the lieutenant stared in surprise. One was a woman; she was dressed in a skirt of gay canvas — once part of an awning of the *Königin Luise* — and a white-linen jacket whose gold buttons and braid showed that it had once belonged to a German naval officer. The other, at whom the lieutenant hardly looked, so astonished was he at sight of a woman, was dressed in a singlet and shorts of the kind worn by German native ratings.

"Get a carrying party," said the lieutenant-commander, proffering no further explanation. "They're pretty far gone."

They were both of them in the feverish stage of malaria, hardly conscious. The lieutenant had them carried up on shore, each in the bight of a blanket, and looked round helplessly to see what he could do with them. In the end he had to lay them in one of the tents allotted to the English sailors, for Port Albert is only a collection of filthy native huts.

"They'll be all right in an hour or two," said the surgeon lieutenant after examining them.

"Christ knows what I'm going to do with 'em," said the lieutenant-commander bitterly. "This isn't the place for sick women."

"Who the devil is she?" asked the lieutenant.

"Some missionary woman or other. The *Königin Luise* found her castaway somewhere on the lake, trying to escape over here."

"Pretty decent of the Huns to bring 'em over."

"Yes," said the lieutenant-commander shortly. It was all very well for a junior officer to say that; he was not harassed as was the lieutenant-commander by constant problems of housing and rations and medical supplies — by all the knotty points in fact which beset a man in command of a force whose lines of communication are a thousand miles long.

"They may be able to give us a bit of useful information about the Huns," said the lieutenant.

"Can we ask them?" interposed the surgeon. "Flag of truce and all that. I don't know the etiquette of these things."

"Oh, you can ask them, all right," said the lieutenant-commander. "There's nothing against it. But you won't get any good out of 'em. I've never met a female devil-dodger yet who was any more use than a sick headache."

And when the officers came to question Rose and All-nutt about the German military arrangements they found, indeed, that they had very little to tell them. Von Hanneken had ringed himself about with desert, and had mobilized every man and woman so as to be ready to strike back at any force which came to molest him, but that the English knew already. The surgeon asked with professional interest about the extent of sleeping sickness among the German forces, but they could tell him nothing about that. The lieutenant wanted to know details of the *Königin Luise*'s crew and equipment; neither Allnutt nor Rose could tell him more than he knew already, more than the Admiralty and the Belgian Government had told him.

The lieutenant-commander looked for a moment beyond the battle which would decide the mastery of the Lake, to the future when a fleet of dhows escorted by the motor boats would take over an invading army which would settle Von Hanneken for good and all. He asked if the Germans had made any active preparations to resist a landing on their shore of the Lake.

"Didn't see nothing," said Allnutt.

Rose understood the drift of the question better.

"You couldn't land anyone where we came from," she said. "It's just a delta — all mud and weed and malaria. It doesn't lead to anywhere."

"No," agreed the lieutenant-commander, who, like an intelligent officer, had studied the technique of combined operations. "I don't think I could, if it's like that. How did you get down to the Lake, then?"

The question was only one of politeness.

"We came down the Ulanga River," said Rose.

"Really?" It was not a matter of great interest to the lieutenant-commander. "I didn't know it was navigable."

"It ain't. Corblimey, it ain't," said Allnutt.

He would not be more explicit about it; the wells of his loquacity were dried up by these glittering officers in their white uniforms with their gentlemen's voices and la-di-da manners. Rose was awkward too. She did not feel at ease with these real gentlemen either, and she was sullenly angry with herself because of the absurd anticlimax in which all her high hopes and high endeavour had ended. Naturally she did not know who the officers were who were questioning her, nor what weapons they were making ready to wield. Naval officers on the eve of an important enterprise would not explain themselves to casual strangers.

"That's interesting," said the lieutenant-commander, in tones which were not in agreement with his words. "You must let me hear about it later on."

He was to be excused for his lack of interest in the petty adventures of these two excessively ordinary people who had made fools of themselves by losing their boat. Tomorrow he had to lead a fleet into action, achieving at this early age the ambition of every naval officer, and he had much to think about.

In fact he had everything to think about.

"They may be all right," said he when they came away. "They look like it. But on the other hand they may not. All this may be just a stunt of old Von Hanneken's to get a couple of his friends over here. I wouldn't put it past him. They're not coming out of their tents until the *Königin Luise* is sunk. They don't seem to be married, and although they've lived together all those weeks it wouldn't be decent if the Royal Navy stuck them in a tent together. I can't really spare another tent. I won't have the camp arrangements jiggered up any more than they are. As it is I've got to take a man off the work to act sentry over them. Can't trust these Belgian natives. Not a ha'p'orth. You see to it, Bones, old man, will you? I've got to go and have a look at *Matilda*'s gun mounting."

Chapter 18

⬤⬤⬤

THE next day the *Königin Luise* as she steamed in solemn dignity over the lake she had ruled so long saw two long grey shapes come hurtling over the water towards her, half-screened in a smother of spray. The commander who had been President of the court martial of two days before looked at them through his glasses as they tore along straight towards him. Beyond the high-tossed bow waves he could see two fluttering squares of white. He saw red crosses and a flash of gay colour in the upper corners. They were White Ensigns, flying where no White Ensign had ever been seen before.

"Action stations!" he snapped. "Get that gun firing!"

The prosecuting officer ran madly to the gun; the defending officer sprang to the wheel to oversee the coloured quartermaster and to make sure the commander's orders were promptly obeyed. Round came the *Königin Luise* to face her enemies. Her feeble gun spoke once, twice, with pitiful slowness. *H.M.S. Matilda* and *H.M.S. Amelia* swerved to one side. At thirty knots they came tearing round in a wide sweep, just outside the longest range of that old six-pounder. The *Königin Luise* was slow on her helm and with a vast turning circle. She could not wheel quick enough to keep her bows towards those flying grey shapes which swept round her in a decreasing spiral. Their engines roared to full throttle as they heeled over on the turn. They had four times the speed and ten times the handiness of the old gunboat. The prosecuting officer looking over his sights could see only their boiling wake now. He could train the gun no farther round, and the gunboat could turn no faster.

The lieutenant-commander stood amidships in the *Matilda.* A thirty-knot gale howled past his ears. The engine bellowed fit to deafen him, but he eyed coolly the lessening range between him and the *Königin Luise,* and the curving course which was bringing his ship fast towards the enemy's stern where there was no gun to bear. It was his duty not merely to win the easy victory, but to see that victory was won at the smallest cost. He looked back to see that the *Amelia* was in her proper station, looked at the range again, shouted an order into the ear of the man at the wheel, and then waved his hand to the sub-lieutenant in the bows by the gun. The three-pounder broke into staccato firing, report following report so that the ear could hardly distinguish one sound from the next. It was a vicious, spiteful sound, implying untold menace and danger.

The three-pounder shells began to burst about the *Königin Luise*'s stern. At first they merely blew holes in the thin plating, and then soon there was no plating left to explode them, and they flew on into the bowels of the ship spreading destruction and fire everywhere, each of them two pounds of flying metal and a pound of high explosive. The steering gear was smashed to fragments, and the *Königin Luise* swerved back suddenly from her circling course and headed on in a wavering straight line. The lieutenant-commander in the *Matilda* gave a new order to the man at the wheel, and kept his boats dead astern, and from that safe position sent the deadly little shells raking through and through the ship from stern to bow.

The *Königin Luise* had not really been designed as a fighting ship; her engines and boilers were above waterline instead of being far below under a protective deck. Soon one of those little shells came flying through the bulkhead, followed by another, and another. There was a deep, sullen roar as the boiler was hit, and the *Königin Luise* was wreathed in a cloud of steam. The engine room staff were boiled alive in that moment.

The lieutenant-commander in the *Matilda* had been expecting that moment; his cool brain had thought of everything. When he saw the steam gush out he gave a quick order, and the roar of the *Matilda*'s engine was stilled as the throttle closed and the engine pulled out of gear. When the steam cleared away the *Königin Luise* was lying a helpless hulk on the water, drifting very slowly with the remnant of her way, and the motor boats were lying silent, still safely astern. He looked for a sign of surrender, but he could see none; the black cross was still flying, challenging the red. Something hit the water beside the *Matilda* with a plop and a jet of water; he could hear a faint crackling from the *Königin Luise*. Some heroic souls there were firing at them with rifles, and even at a mile and a half a Mauser bullet can kill, and on the great lakes of Africa where white men are numbered only in tens, and every white man can lead a hundred black men to battle, white men's lives are precious. He must not expose his sailors to this danger longer than he need.

"Hell," said the lieutenant-commander. He did not want to kill the wretched Germans, who were achieving nothing in prolonging their defence. "God damn it; all right, then."

He shouted an order to the gun's crew in the bows, and the fire recommenced, elevated a little so as to sweep the deck. One shell killed three coloured ratings who were lying on the deck firing with their rifles; the prosecuting officer never knew how he escaped. Another shell burst on the tall bridge, and killed Lieutenant Schumann, but it did not harm the commander, who had gone down below a minute before, venturing with his coat over his face into the scalding steam of the engine room to do his last duty.

"Perhaps that'll settle 'em," said the lieutenant-commander, signalling for fire to cease. Even three-pounder shells are troublesome to replace over lines of communication a thousand miles long. He looked at the *Königin Luise* again. She lay motionless, hazed around with smoke and steam. There was no firing now, but the black-cross flag was still flying, drooping in the still air.

Then the lieutenant-commander saw that she was lower in the water, and as he noticed it the *Königin Luise* very suddenly fell over to one side. The commander had done his duty; he had groped his way through the wrecked engines to the sea-cocks and had opened them.

"Hope we can save the poor beggars," said the lieutenant-commander, calling for full speed.

The *Matilda* and the *Amelia* came rushing up just as the German ensign, the last thing to disappear, dipped below the surface. They were in time to save all the living except the hopelessly wounded.

Chapter 19

⊷

THERE is an elation in victory, even when wounded men have to be borne very carefully along the jetty to the hospital tent; even when a telegraphic report has to be composed and sent to the Lords Commissioners of the Admiralty; even when a lieutenant-commander of no linguistic ability has to put together another report in French for the Belgian governor. He could at least congratulate himself on having won a naval victory as decisive as the Falklands or Tsushima, and he could look forward to receiving the D.S.O. and the Belgian Order of the Crown and a step in promotion which would help to make him an admiral some day.

His mind was already hard at work on his new plans, busily anticipating the time soon to come when he would escort the invading army across the lake. "Strike quickly, strike hard, and keep on striking"; the sooner the invaders were on their way the less time would Von

Hanneken have to recover from this totally unexpected blow and make arrangements to oppose a landing. The lieutenant-commander was urgent in his representations to the senior Belgian officer on the spot, to the Belgian headquarters, to the British headquarters in East Africa.

Yet meanwhile he could not be free from the worry of all commanders-in-chief. That long line of communications was a dreadful nuisance, and he had fifty blue jackets who expected English rations in Central Africa, and now he had some captured German wounded — coloured men mostly, it is true, but a drain on his resources all the same — on his hands as well as some unwounded prisoners. He had to act promptly in the matter. He sent for Rose and Allnutt.

"There's a Belgian escort going down to the coast with prisoners," he said, shortly. "I'm going to send you with them. That will be all right for you, I suppose."

"I suppose so," said Allnutt. Until this moment they had been people without a future. Even the destruction of the *Königin Luise* had increased that feeling of nothingness ahead.

"You'll be going to join up, I suppose," said the lieutenant-commander. "I can't enlist you here, of course. I can't do anything about it. But down on the coast you'll find a British consul, at Matadi, I think, or somewhere there. The Belgians'll put you on the right track, anyway. Any British consul will do your business for you. As soon as you are over your malaria, of course. They'll send you round to join one of the South African units, I expect. So you'll be all right."

"Yessir," said Allnutt.

"And you, Mrs. — er — Miss Sayer, isn't it?" went on the lieutenant-commander. "I think the West Coast's the best solution of the problem for you, too, don't you? You can get back to England from there. A British consul —"

"Yes," said Rose.

"That's all right then," said the lieutenant-commander with relief. "You'll be starting in two or three hours."

It was hard to expect a young officer planning the conquest of a country half the size of Europe to devote more attention to two civilian castaways. It was that "Mrs. — er — Miss" of the lieutenant-commander's which really settled Rose's future — or unsettled it, if that view be taken. When they came out of the lieutenant-commander's presence Rose was seething with shame. Until then she had been a woman without a future and in consequence without any real care. It was different now. The lieutenant-commander had mentioned the possibility of a return to England; to Rose that meant a picture of poor streets and censorious people and prying aunts — that aunts should be prying was in Rose's experience an essential characteristic of aunts. And it was terribly painful to contemplate a separation from Allnutt; he had been so much to her; she had hardly been out of his sight for weeks now; to lose him now would be like losing a limb, even if her feelings towards him had changed; she could not contemplate this unforeseen future of hers without Allnutt.

"Charlie," she said urgently. "We've got to get married."

"Coo," said Allnutt. This was an aspect of the situation he actually had not thought of.

"We must do it as quickly as we can," said Rose. "A consul can marry people. That officer in there spoke about a consul. As soon as we get to the coast . . ."

Allnutt was a little dazed and stupid. This unlooked-for transfer to the West Coast of Africa, this taken-for-granted enlistment in the South African forces, and now this new proposal left him with hardly a word to say. He thought of Rose's moderate superiority in social status. He thought about money; presumably he would receive pay in the South African army. He thought about the girl he had married twelve years ago when he was eighteen. She had probably been through half a dozen men's hands by now, but there had never been a divorce and presumably he was still married to her. Oh well, South Africa and England were a long way apart, and she couldn't trouble him much.

"Righto, Rosie," he said, "let's."

So they left the lakes and began the long journey to Matadi and marriage. Whether or not they lived happily ever after is not easily decided.

In praise of C. S. Forester's
Horatio Hornblower novels

Mr. Midshipman Hornblower

"English naval history comes truly alive. . . . The historical novel is rarely so well served."
  —*Times Literary Supplement* (London)

Lieutenant Hornblower

"Sound history, absorbing adventure, and spanking good writing." — *Chicago Tribune*

Hornblower and the Hotspur

"In storm, in flame, in blood, and in love, the plot unfolds."
  — *Christian Science Monitor*

"No other contemporary writer can equal Forester at this kind of storytelling." — *Chicago Tribune*

Hornblower During the Crisis

"A first-rate swashbuckler." — *New York Times Book Review*

"Told with impeccable, salty craftsmanship and a fine, bracing conviction that history needs to be improved upon." — *Time*

Hornblower and the Atropos

"Delightful . . . everlastingly entertaining." — *Saturday Review*

"C. S. Forester's knowledge of the technical side of life during the Napoleonic Wars is a continual delight."
  — *Times Literary Supplement* (London)

Beat to Quarters

"The best account of an engagement at sea that I have ever read. . . . In a class by itself."

  —James Norman Hall, coauthor of *Mutiny on the Bounty*

"As gripping and realistic a sea tale as you are likely to run across." — *New York Times*

more . . .

www.ingramcontent.com/pod-product-compliance
Lightning Source LLC
LaVergne TN
LVHW032033250625
814609LV00007B/307